# Where Love Lives

## A Later in Life Romance

### Waterstead Love Story Trilogy
#### Book 2

## Eliza Ester

 Created with Vellum

Hey there romance reader!

I'm glad you've stumbled across this page.
Did you know that I have a newsletter where I share my new releases, book discounts and other goodies that I hear about in the romance genre?

You can sign up at the website below and you may just hear me yell with joy wherever you happen to be. :)
Eliza


www.ElizaEster.com/

# Chapter 1
# Fern

Fern tugged at her loose cotton blouse and fanned herself against the heat. It was barely nine in the morning, and the little town of Waterstead was already an oven. But that was Texas weather at its finest. Fern had grown up with it, and she wouldn't trade the blazing heat for snow or wind or anything else.

She loved it here.

While she waited in front of V Studios, she glanced around as the sleepy town came to life. Until she'd answered the ad for an artist's assistant in Waterstead, she'd never heard of the place. And no surprise—the town was just a sliver. It was sandwiched between Carlos Bay and Saint Charles Bay on a slim finger of land and shared a border with the Arkansas National Wildlife Rescue.

Despite being across the water from places like Holiday Beach, Rockport, and the greater Arkansas Bay, Waterstead was out of the way, quiet, and almost forgotten. It was a nice change of pace from the oversized, overcrowded, over-everything Houston.

Fern scowled when she thought about her hometown.

She'd always loved the city. There was so much to do, so much to see, so many opportunities to take. But with so much space for good, there was also that much space for bad, and it was the bad that Fern had fled from.

The ad on her phone had been a godsend.

An old car pulled up, and the driver turned the ignition off. A woman with dark hair stepped out of the car.

"I'm sorry I'm late," she breathed. "We had an...incident at home. I'm Veronica Tellez." She walked to Fern with her hand extended. Fern glanced down at Veronica's black shirt, riddled with dog hair.

"Nothing too serious, I hope?" she asked, glancing into Veronica's dark eyes. "Fern Cantu." She shook Veronica's hand warmly.

"Oh no." Veronica laughed. "We have a dog on the property—Buster—and he can be adamant not to let me leave when the mood for cuddles hits him."

Fern grinned. "Let me guess. That mood for cuddles happens...all the time."

"You better believe it." Veronica laughed. "Do you have dogs?"

Fern shook her head, a shadow of bitterness creeping in. She pushed it aside. She wasn't going to think about anything that would put her in a bad mood. She was here for an interview, and first impressions mattered.

If this was how it started off—relaxed and full of laughter, with Veronica looking like she'd brought half a farm with her —then Fern was sure she could relax a little, too. The tension was already starting to bleed from her shoulders, and Veronica's warmth coaxed a smile out of her.

"Let me show you what you'll be working with," Veronica said, unlocking the door to the studio.

The wooden building looked like it was stuck somewhere in the sands of time. It needed a bit of work and attention, maybe a lick of paint, but it was an old building. Nostalgia clung to its walls as they walked in.

"Oh, what a wonderful space!" Fern cried out as she took in the large display room they stood in.

Art pieces hung on the wall, some displayed on pedestals in the center of the room, and large windows let in tons of natural light. The sun cast its morning light into the windows, setting the paintings on fire with splashes of gold.

"Oh, yes," Fern gushed. "There's magic in here."

Veronica smiled. "Magic?"

Fern glanced at her. "Some places just allow for creativity. I don't know what it is, but when it happens—like in this room —it's so much easier to make art. To let the colors choose themselves and the painting come to life."

Veronica continued to smile at Fern, and Fern blushed. "I know it sounds a little crazy," she said quickly. "But art can really be a live thing, you know?"

"I know!" Veronica agreed. "I feel the same way. And since I bought this place, I've been painting like crazy. I was out of it for a long time...but the moment I picked up a brush, it just broke that damn wall, and it's been flowing ever since."

Fern smiled. "That's exactly what I mean." She was glad someone understood.

Art was Fern's savior. When the world had felt dark and dreary, she'd always been able to mix the right colors to bring light back into it. Painting was an escape whenever the weight of the world got too heavy.

And when the world became ugly, she could paint her way back to the beautiful things that mattered.

"I'm so glad you feel that way about painting," Veronica said. "I want the person who works here to feel the same passion for art as I do. It looks like you have it, and it's just what I need. And your students will draw inspiration from that kind of passion, too."

Fern smiled, but her stomach twisted a little. "You keep talking as if the job is already mine."

Veronica frowned. "Don't you want it?"

"Oh, of course I do. I just...this is an interview, right? To find out if you like me enough to work here?"

"Right," Veronica said. "I suppose I should ask you some questions." She leaned against a tall counter in the corner where a few books and files were stacked. If this was the total of their administration department—Fern giggled inwardly at that wording—there was a bit of work to be done.

But first, the interview.

Veronica tapped a finger to her chin, glancing toward the ceiling as she thought. She seemed a little ditzy, as if her mind was somewhere else and jumping around all the time. Fern had been around erratic people often; in fact, they were the definition of her life, with her mom's illness and Hank...

Fern shoved the thoughts into a box and locked it up tight. She refused to let her situation at home, the way she grew up, drag her down so much that she missed a great opportunity.

And Veronica was nothing like them. Her scattered behavior was endearing. Fern didn't know what it was about the dark-haired woman, but she liked her.

"You're from Houston, right?" Veronica asked. "It's a big move to come all the way out here."

Fern nodded. "Sometimes we have nothing left but to make a big change, you know?"

"Oh, I know all about that," Veronica said softly. She gazed toward a window, her eyes changing as if she was looking at something far away. Or as if she was looking into the past, at something long gone.

"What kind of experience do you have, other than what you listed for me in your resume?" Veronica suddenly asked, her attention snapping back to the present. For a moment, her eyes appeared to shimmer with unshed tears, but when she blinked, they were gone.

"Well, that's a tough question to answer," Fern said. "Aside from my years of painting and a few online courses here and there, I'm mostly self-taught. I know it means I don't have all the qualifications." She swallowed hard. Her lack of qualifications was what made this job application such a risk. Dragging her whole life here for a job she might not get had drained most of her savings. "But that only means I have what it takes to be a trailblazer. Everything I know, I taught myself and practiced and tried until I found what worked. The other upside is that I don't have the strict rules that come with professional teaching. I only paint what I feel, not what I *know*. And that counts for something. It's so important to let art come to life and be what it wants to be, right?"

Veronica smiled. While Fern spoke, it had been hard to read the older woman. She had a solid poker face, and that made Fern nervous. She preferred being around people she could easily read so she knew when to get away from them to protect herself—and save herself.

*You're far from Houston and the hell you call home. Not everything is a fight for survival out here.*

Veronica's eyes softened, her expressionless mask cracking and giving way to a beaming smile. "You sound perfect for the job."

Fern laughed. "You're sure?"

"Yes! Sometimes fate sends the right people on your path, and questioning it only makes life harder for yourself. I know this from experience by now." She smirked before she shrugged. "I've learned to roll with the punches. When can you start?"

"Right away," Fern said. "What will my duties be?"

Veronica frowned, a map of lines appearing on her brow.

"Oh...I don't know."

Fern frowned. "You don't know?"

Veronica giggled nervously. "You're my very first employee. I knew I needed help with the studio, so I put out the ad, but as for duties…" She swallowed hard.

Fern smiled. This was the perfect time to show Veronica what she had in mind. There was nothing like making a great first impression.

"What do you need help with?" she asked. "Let's start there."

"Well, I need someone to man the shop when I'm away. And I need someone to teach classes. There are a few things that need to be done around here, so someone who's hands-on and always available is a must."

Fern nodded, confident in herself and her abilities now that the tension had been broken and she knew she'd gotten the job. She reeled inside, the excitement bubbling through her veins. Just like that, she'd been hired! But she kept her professional mask in place.

After Veronica left, she would do a little dance of excitement and squeal with delight.

"I've got this," Fern said, nodding. "I'm great with people, and I'm an excellent teacher because I taught myself. There's no education like making all the mistakes yourself and learning from them."

She was blowing her own horn now, but it felt so good to be in this creative space, to be understood by someone, even if it was just one part of her life. And the more time Fern spent with Veronica, the more she liked her.

"I'm so glad you're on board," Veronica said, beaming again. "Let me get that down." She grabbed a sheet of paper and a charcoal pencil—the only writing tool lying around. The pencil was so fitting in an art studio, Fern couldn't help but smile.

While Veronica wrote, Fern studied her. She was a little

older than Fern's thirty-eight years, and she looked like she'd been through a lot in her life. But she'd gotten through it, and that inner light of hers still shone. As long as that little light still burned, Fern believed there was still hope—for anyone.

It was when that light went out that things became terrible.

She'd seen it happen, and she didn't wish that kind of pain and suffering that snuffed out that light on anyone she knew.

Not even Hank, one of the reasons her life had been so tough growing up.

*Don't think about them, think about the goodness that lies ahead. There's no use looking back. You can't change the past. Keep looking forward. The future can still be golden.*

"Right," Veronica said, looking at her scribbles. They were barely legible, scrawled as they were in the thick charcoal pencil, but they were good enough. She cleared her throat. "Day-to-day operations and teaching classes. That about sums it up as far as your duties go, don't you think?"

Fern nodded. "And the first Artist-in-Residence."

Veronica blinked at her, confused. "What?"

Fern's cheeks reddened, and she squirmed inwardly. This was when she was sure Veronica would throw her out, but she had to take the chance. Waterstead had very few places available to live long-term, and if Fern didn't find a home here, she didn't know what she would do.

She felt like a ship lost at sea, and a life in Waterstead was the anchor she desperately needed.

"Well, I did my research about the town after I heard about it the first time..." she offered a bashful smile.

"Yeah, this place is very out of the way, huh?" Veronica said. "So close to the real world, and still it's removed and stuck in a fairytale land of its own."

Fern chuckled. That was the perfect way to put it. "I've

done my research, and I happen to know the apartment above the studio is empty. So, I figured if you let me, I can live in it."

Veronica hesitated. "That's not what I'm hiring for."

Fern had to talk fast, feeling the opportunity slip through her fingers.

"I moved all the way from Houston for this job. I know it sounds crazy, but I threw everything I own into my car, rented an Airbnb for a week, driving to this forgotten town to start over. I can't..." Her tongue suddenly felt thick, and more emotion overcame her than she was ready to show. She fought to keep it together. "I can't let it end in nothing."

It was a weak finish. She'd wanted to communicate so much more.

Veronica's face softened. "I know all about starting over when you feel like it's all too much. Trust me, it's the hardest thing you'll ever do. But it can also be the best thing." She nodded to herself, as if she'd come to a conclusion. "And you're right—the studio apartment upstairs is empty. It will help me if someone's here to open the shop in the morning and lock up in the evening. I think it's a great idea."

"You do?" Fern asked, trying to hide her surprise.

"You bet," Veronica said with a wide grin. "I like the initiative, Fern. That's what I'm looking for around here."

A rush of warmth traveled through Fern.

"Come on, let's go look at the apartment," Veronica said. "It's a mess up there. Since getting this place, I've been trying to figure it all out, but it's come together so fast."

"Really?"

"The sale and transfer only happened a few months ago, and I'm still finding my feet in this small town. It's more of a home than I've felt in a long time, but it's still an adventure."

Veronica and Fern walked through the door to the shop and around the side of the wooden building. Stairs led to the first floor, and Veronica unlocked a rickety door that creaked wildly when she swung it open.

"I've only been up here once," Veronica said apologetically. "I live down by the waterside, so I haven't had a reason—or the time—to rummage through the junk up here."

"I can help with cleaning," Fern offered as she stepped through the front door to the studio apartment.

They stood in a small foyer, and Veronica unlocked a second door. Fern liked the idea of having two doors and an added layer of security. If someone came up unexpectedly, she'd hear them before they were on her.

"Oh no," Veronica said, rattling the doorknob. The door remained shut. "I think it's stuck."

"Let me try," Fern suggested, and she rattled the door in the same way. Nothing happened.

"We might have to ram it open," Veronica said thoughtfully.

"What?"

"You and me," Veronica said, determined. "We'll shoulder it together. We're not very big, and you're a slight thing..." Her eyes wandered down Fern's body and back up again. "But we can do it together. Girl power, right?" She laughed.

"Right," Fern said. "Let's do it."

They positioned themselves against the door, facing each other. Veronica had her hand on the doorknob.

"Ready?" she asked.

Fern nodded, and they both shouldered the door at the same time.

"Ow!" Veronica cried out, rubbing her shoulder.

Fern winced and did the same. The door was stuck, and ramming against it had *hurt*.

"I think I felt it budge," Fern said.

"Did you?"

Fern nodded. "Maybe one more time."

"It better open," Veronica grumbled. "Thatcher will wonder why I'm purple and blue."

"Thatcher?" Fern asked.

Veronica smiled, her face lighting up like a Christmas tree. "He's my boyfriend."

"Ah," Fern said. "Well, better make it worth our while then. One, two, three!"

They shouldered the door another time. When it wouldn't work, they did it again, working together without discussing it.

The door suddenly crashed open, and the two women tumbled into the room with nothing to stop their momentum as the door banged against the wall.

Veronica yelped, and Fern cried out as they fell to the floor with a thud. They lay on the wooden slats panting. When Veronica looked at Fern with eyes wide, they burst out laughing.

"Well, that's one way to do it," Veronica said, pulling herself up. She offered Fern a hand, and together, the two women hoisted themselves to their feet. Fern dusted off her clothes, and Veronica ran a hand through her hair, looking around.

"Oh," Veronica said, her smile fading. "This is a bigger mess than I remember."

Fern followed her gaze. Boxes were stacked all around the room. Veronica and Fern proceeded to open some of the boxes, looking at the contents. They were filled with photographs, letters, journals...the evidence of a life well-lived.

"Oh, wow," Fern breathed, running her fingers over the old stuff. Nostalgia clung to it.

"This is a lot to work through," Veronica said. She dragged a finger along a flat surface, and it came away thick with dust. "And a lot of cleaning to do."

"I don't mind the work," Fern said quickly. "I'll take care

of it. I still have my time at the Airbnb. You won't have to do a thing. I've got it covered." She bit her lower lip. This was what she wanted—to live here, to work here, to learn how to breathe again here. If she had to work to make it happen, she would do it. Whatever it took.

"I'm not taking the job away from you," Veronica said with a smile. "I meant what I said about fate. I think you're meant to be here, just like I am, and we'll figure this out. But your offer to clean up is great." She walked to Fern and squeezed her hand with a big smile on her face. "Welcome to Waterstead!"

"Oh!" Fern cried out, suddenly emotional. Everything was falling into place. "Thank you!"

Veronica grabbed Fern into a hug, and the woman allowed the affection. It had been a while since she'd felt like she belonged somewhere, accepted without question.

Leaving Houston had been scary. But it had been the right thing to do.

This was the start of something beautiful.

# Chapter 2
# Elliot

"Hey, Elli," Tina said.

On the other side of the line, Elliot grinned at the nickname. He wouldn't allow anyone else to call him that, but he'd always had a soft spot for his sister.

"I'm just calling to check in, see how you're doing," he said.

"You don't have to call me every day, you know," Tina said. "I'm not in a bad space anymore."

Elliot nodded. Tina was better off now that they'd managed to get rid of her abusive husband, but he still worried about her. It would be a long time before he stopped checking in with her every day. She'd been hurt too much, and Elliot wanted to be there for her if something was wrong.

"I know," he said. "But I miss your face."

"Liar." She giggled.

"It's true. I don't know how I'll survive when I leave."

Tina sighed heavily. "And you're still set on that?"

Elliot's heart sank as he talked about leaving his life—and his sister—in Rockport behind to start a new life in a big city somewhere. But it had to be done. It was the only way he could imagine expanding his growing business, and he wanted to get away from this small town.

"I think it's the best thing I can do for the business," he said.

"And to get away from Mom and Dad," Tina pointed out.

"It's not about that," Elliot protested, but his sister was right, even when he didn't want to admit to it. He wanted to get away from the proof that love could die. He hated being around his parents now, hearing how much each hated the other and had wasted their best years on a relationship that meant nothing. It was enough to put Elliot off dating for good.

Leaving Rockport was the best thing he could do. He could always come back to visit, right? Or fly Tina out to see him. It would be a new adventure, and who didn't love adventures?

"How are things with work?" Tina asked, and Elliot was grateful for the change of topic. Tina knew when it was tough for him to talk about something.

"Good. I've taken one last contract in Waterstead before I go."

"Oh, that sounds cool," Tina said. "It's that weird little town across the bay, right?"

"Right," Elliot said with a laugh. "I'm staying there for a few days to take care of it, but you know you can call me anytime, and I'll be right back."

Elliot could almost see his sister rolling her eyes. "I'll be fine, Elliot. Really. Have fun! And see it as a holiday or something. A break away from Rockport."

"I'll just be trading one small coastal town for another, even smaller coastal town," Elliot remarked.

He would be glad when he was finally gone. Everyone always talked about how it was their dream to move to the coast and settle down, but he'd had that all his life. He just wanted to get away and settle into a big city where everyone didn't know everyone, where no one knew about the marital problems his parents had. He just wanted to break free and start over.

"I have to go," Elliot said. "I'll talk to you soon."

"Have fun, okay?" Tina said.

"I'll be working with my hands again for a change. I can't think of anything more fun than that."

Tina giggled before he ended the call, and he grinned. Elliot loved his sister and would miss her when he left. He was serious about what he'd said about enjoying working with his hands. He'd started his company as a handyman and builder a long time ago, working hard as the only one in his business until he'd been able to expand it so much, he had a whole crew of men working under him now. He would have to tell them he was moving soon, too. He would have to lay them off, and that didn't sit well with him. He couldn't expect them to want to relocate with him...

He shook off those thoughts. He would worry about things like that later. First, he had to settle on where he wanted to be, and then he could take the next step. He'd approached a real estate agent who was selecting various places for him, and he expected a call from her soon.

Until then, he would do this job in the small town, relish working with his hands again, and trust that the rest of it would fall into place.

He loaded equipment and supplies into the back of his truck before he got behind the wheel and drove out of Rockport. Waterstead wasn't very far away, and Elliot soon arrived at the quaint little town. It looked like the town had escaped from a storybook.

Following the directions Thatcher Hoskins had sent him, Elliot turned onto the dirt driveway on one of the last roads against the water. Everything about Waterstead had impressed him since the moment he'd driven into the town. Quaint and picturesque, it was the perfect ideal of a waterside town that seemed to have gotten lost in time somewhere. Here, the hustle and bustle of the real world didn't exist, and the peace and quiet was almost overwhelming.

Elliot glanced at the wooden structure built on stilts near the water's edge. With his trained eye, it wasn't hard to tell that this place would require a lot of work. He had his work cut out for him, but he was the best in the business, tinkering, repairing, and restoring what had once been beautiful.

He stood with his hands on his hips. The house, beautiful as it was with its large windows and covered porch that looked out over the ocean, had sat down on itself as if it was tired from years and years of holding itself up.

He walked toward the house and climbed the rickety stairs that creaked and groaned dangerously with every step he took. The cottage he spied in the background seemed to be in better condition. Still, he wouldn't know the extent of the work until—

A loud bark sliced through his train of thought. Then another loud bark, deep and rumbling. A moment later, the biggest dog he'd ever seen skidded around the corner, nails clattering on the wooden porch. The large ball of fur shot right at him.

"Oh, look at you!" Elliot cried out. It was one of the biggest, most beautiful Saint Bernards Elliot had seen in a long time.

The dog barked again and lunged toward Elliot.

Elliot had expected it—he was no stranger to big dogs— and braced himself. When the dog jumped on him, he grabbed onto the dog's collar but didn't yank him down.

"You're just a big sweetheart, aren't you?" Elliot asked when the dog started licking his face with a large pink tongue. Standing on its hind legs with its front legs against Elliot's chest, the dog reached his face with ease. "Well, I don't have to ask who's in charge around here."

"Buster!" a voice shouted from inside.

"Uh oh. Look like you're in trouble, huh?" Elliot said to the dog with a chuckle.

"Buster, get off him! We do *not* jump on guests!"

A man yanked open the screen door and stepped out. He was tall and on the thinner side with an easy way about him.

"Down, boy," he admonished. He didn't look like he could wrestle down the animal. Elliot was impressed that Thatcher—he assumed that was who this man was—didn't yank the dog down or punish him. He only talked sternly to him.

Buster whined, shaking his head, but obeyed his master and dropped his large body back to all fours.

"Sorry about that," Thatcher said, scratching Buster behind the ears when he plopped down on the wooden boards with a sigh, panting. "He's just a big teddy bear. He doesn't usually like people, but lately, he's been surprising me with who he lets into our lives."

"Dogs are excellent judges of character," Elliot said. "I'll trust a dog's judgment far more than any human's."

"You sound like the kind of man I can get along with," Thatcher said with a grin and held out his hand. "Sorry for the rude introduction. I'm Thatcher Hoskins."

"Elliot Garner. I made it a little earlier than expected. The drive from Rockport was surprisingly fast."

"It's deceivingly close, huh?" Thatcher said. "I'm glad you made it."

Elliot nodded. His business in Rockport—Handyman with Heart—did well enough that he'd started advertising in the greater Copano Bay area. He glanced at the house.

"It's a gem you've got here," he said. "But it might take a

bit of work to really patch the place up and restore it to its former glory."

"That's why you're here," Thatcher said. He lifted a hand to his forehead as if he was used to wearing a hat. "I was going to fix the place up myself, but it's a lot more work than I bargained for. Besides, life got in the way, and I got busy."

"It happens to the best of us," Elliot said with a smile.

He liked Thatcher's easy-going attitude. He was just a client right now, but Elliot imagined Thatcher was the type of guy he could enjoy a cold beer with at sunset.

Elliot didn't have a lot of friends. He had people he invited to important gatherings, but no one he could confide in, reveal his hopes and dreams to, or confess his fears to. No one aside from Tina, and after what she'd been through, he was careful not to burden her with things in his life when she had so much to deal with already.

Sometimes, he wished he had friends...

What was going on with him? He didn't usually think too much about his position in life. There was no use complaining about something that wouldn't change, and Elliot had learned a long time ago that the key to happiness was finding the good in every situation rather than complaining about it.

*Come on now, this is a client. Be professional.*

"Let's have a look at what we're working with," Elliot said, getting right down to business.

"It's a big one," Thatcher warned.

"Luckily, I'm good at my job, and I don't shy away from a challenge," Elliot said.

Thatcher grinned. His blue eyes were kind. He beckoned Elliot to follow him into the house.

It was a beautiful house, clearly built by someone who wanted to draw all the attention to the private beach that ran along the back of the property. The large windows and covered porch offered incredible views, and the bedrooms were all spacious. This wasn't just a home; it was a sanctuary.

One that seemed to be falling apart.

Buster walked with them, his nails clicking on the wooden floors, tail wagging against everything, knocking things over.

"He's going to be our entourage all day," Thatcher said unapologetically.

"It's the only way to see the house," Elliot said gravely before he grinned. "Three's a party."

Thatcher laughed. "With Buster, everything's a party."

As they moved from room to room, Thatcher explained everything he needed done—plumbing, electricity, gas connections, built-in cupboards, a new ceiling in one of the bedrooms, water damage against a bathroom wall. His list of requirements was just short of rebuilding the house from scratch. And it wasn't just the main house, either. Thatcher wanted work done on the cottage, too, though it was in a much better state. The work it needed could be tacked on almost as an afterthought.

The main house would be the biggest project.

"You were planning to do all this by yourself?" Elliot asked, scratching his head. His mind spun with numbers so he could quote Thatcher the job that needed to be done, but it was going to amount to a lot more than he wanted to say out loud.

"Yeah," Thatcher said, rubbing the back of his neck, his other hand on his hip. "But life throws all kinds of curveballs at you. First, it was the woman of my dreams." He cocked a smile that could only be one of a man in love. "And then a great business opportunity. The Reserve next door asked me to help with a couple of things, and I realized I'm better at natural preservation than I realized. All my years on the ranch gave me insight no one else has, apparently. Suddenly, I have my hands full with work, and the burning desire to *not* take ten years to rebuild this place myself."

Elliot was glad Thatcher had said "rebuild." It meant the man understood what kind of work had to go into the house. He also felt a pang of envy that this man had been able to start over, his life going in a new direction without him looking for it, per se. But no one who made it this far in life had it easy, and Elliot was sure Thatcher had paid his dues.

They all had their path to walk, didn't they? Elliot was on his own path, and he would reach his destination in time, too. All in good time. It just took a bit of work, a lot of patience, and the good sense to take an opportunity when it presented itself without letting fear get in the way.

That last part was the most challenging, but after Elliot's thirty-nine years of life, he'd started to realize that fear only did one thing—held him back. He was determined not to be held back by something as simple as his worry that something might not work out. How many times had he had to pick himself up again? Everyone made mistakes, everyone fell. As long as he could pick himself back up and keep going, there wasn't anything that could go so wrong that he couldn't find a silver lining, a way to get out on the other end.

That wasn't a skill he'd learned from his cold, harsh father, that was for sure. Maybe it was *because* of his father that Elliot had learned to do it. He figured he could either let his past define him, or let it shape him like a pebble in a stream until he was smooth and round and complete. A work of art.

"So, what do you think?" Thatcher asked.

Elliot abandoned his train of thought, coming back to the present. Why was he so caught up in the past today? He usually pushed it all away and focused on moving forward. Something about this town allowed him to go back in time and revisit the past. He wasn't sure how he felt about that.

Thatcher looked eager, rubbing his hands together. "Do you feel up to the job?"

They stood on the lawn that overlooked the beach, with a path leading down to it. Suddenly, Elliot felt an incredible urge to kick off his shoes and dig his feet into the sand. Buster was on the beach, running back and forth, barking at seagulls. He looked so free, Elliot wondered what Thatcher would think if he joined the dog and did the same. The thought of him on the beach, running around like a lunatic, was amusing. He would look like an idiot, so he fought the temptation. But the beach was inviting.

He forced himself to focus on business. Thatcher had asked a question, and Elliot nodded slowly. "It's not an impossible feat. Let's start there."

"But?" Thatcher asked.

"How much did you budget for the project?" Elliot asked.

Thatcher told him a number. Elliot swallowed hard.

"What can I realistically expect with that kind of money?" Thatcher asked.

The sound of the waves crashing on the sand was welcoming, and the breeze picked up, bringing a bit of relief from the pressing heat.

"I'm going to be honest with you," Elliot said. "The estimate for a job this big will blow away your budget." He offered Thatcher a level stare. There was no point in beating about the bush. The sooner Thatcher knew what to expect, the sooner the man could decide.

It was a lot of money.

Elliot hoped Thatcher would sign up for the job despite the price he quoted him. Not only because his fingers itched to get into something that would inspire and challenge him—he'd become stagnant recently—but because he'd decided he wanted to stick around Waterstead for a while. It was peaceful here. Something about the place made him feel like he could rest his aching soul.

"Hmm," Thatcher said, thinking out loud. "I expected it might be a bit of a challenge." He rubbed his chin where a dark, graying beard was starting to take shape after a few days of not shaving. "Moving here has been my lifelong dream. I bit off more than I could chew by buying this fixer-upper, but I still think this is where I need to be. So, we'll figure it out."

"How did you end up with a property like this?" Elliot asked. "If you don't mind me prying."

"I saw it online and bought it," Thatcher said with a grin. "It was my last hurrah, and I don't regret it. It's given me so much more than I ever bargained for. I'm a rancher from Montana, and I thought it might be too late to change things. But here I am, starting a new life."

"It's never too late to start over," Elliot agreed. "Sometimes, it's what we need to do."

"You get it," Thatcher said. "And there's something about this town that offers hope. They should have called it Hope Springs rather than Waterstead." He chuckled.

"How are you liking Texas so far?" Elliot asked. "Montana is a long way away."

Thatcher nodded. "I love it here, but I think I have it lucky in this small town. I have a feeling this isn't the most Texan town to exist in the state. The people here are all very different, very quirky. And it's a tight-knit community, let me tell you. Everyone is in everyone's business. It's as endearing as it is frustrating."

"I can only imagine," Elliot said. "Rockport is about five times as big as this place. The population here is about two thousand, if I'm correct?"

"If it's even that much," Thatcher said. "I imagine it gets busier during the summer holidays, but we just missed that part. I'm glad about that."

Elliot nodded. "Yeah, your private beach will do you good. You don't have to navigate the tourists."

"Right, right," Thatcher said, pushing his hands into his pockets. "It's the kind of place that draws you in, though. People end up here by chance, and then they stay for a lifetime."

"It sounds like the kind of reset a man might need," Elliot said.

"Oh, you know it," Thatcher said with a grin. "Anyway, I might have to revisit my finances. Could you start on something smaller in the meantime?"

Elliot frowned. "Like what?"

"I own another place in town that doesn't need as much work. Do you have time to check it out with me?"

"Of course," Elliot said. "I set aside the day for this quote, and I'm in town indefinitely. I'm checking into the hotel on the main road later."

"Perfect," Thatcher said with a grin. "Follow me into town. I'll show it to you."

Elliot nodded, getting back into his vehicle. Thatcher popped back into the main house to retrieve his keys before walking to a truck parked under a large tree. Buster padded after him happily.

"You're not coming with me today, Bus," Thatcher said.

Buster tried to get into the open door despite Thatcher's words.

"No, Buster, come on," Thatcher said, wrestling the dog out of the way.

Elliot watched the exchange with a smile. Buster was a character, and he clearly had a mind of his own.

It took Thatcher a good ten minutes to get the dog to back down, and the only way he eventually succeeded was by running into the house and bringing out a rawhide chew toy for Buster to keep himself busy with.

Buster reluctantly accepted the toy, gazing at Thatcher with a hard look that said, "I know you're just trying to trick me into staying behind, and I'm going to allow it only because I want this toy. But this isn't over yet."

Elliot laughed when Thatcher gave him an exasperated look and walked to Elliot's vehicle to talk to him.

"Sometimes he's quicker than others, but he's full of it today. He didn't want to let Veronica, my girlfriend, leave, either. I had to wrestle Buster to the ground this morning just so she could go to work!"

Elliot chuckled.

"But I wouldn't have it any other way. Life would be so dull without him. Are you ready to go?"

"Ready."

Thatcher walked to his truck, hopping in quickly in case Buster changed his mind about staying behind.

They left the property, and Elliot glanced at it in the rearview mirror. As much as he loved it, he knew it was going to be a lot of hard work. But Elliot was no stranger to hard work. It was the only way to get where he wanted in life, and it had helped him escape the pain in his reality. He only worried that the project, with whatever extra property Thatcher was about to show him now, would become so big that Thatcher couldn't afford it.

But Thatcher looked like a man with a solid head on his shoulders. Elliot had to trust that he was in the right place at the right time. If the comfortable way he and Thatcher had chatted was anything to go by, Elliot wanted to stick around a while longer.

Waterstead was nothing like the chaos in his life, and it seemed like the perfect ending to this chapter before he started a new life somewhere else.

# Chapter 3
## Fern

The studio apartment was small, but it was beautiful. Fern pictured it with all the rubble removed and cleaned, with the few pieces of furniture dusted and moved into the right places. This room could really sing, and Fern knew she could be happy here. All she needed was a bit of work, but hard work was something she could do. She'd worked her whole life to create a life for herself. She'd faced every adversity she could possibly imagine, and she'd come out on the other side.

"Where did you say you're staying?" Veronica asked after they'd poked around in the old boxes.

"Just behind the haberdashery, if that's any help," Fern said.

Veronica nodded. "I know where that is. My friend Linda owns the shop. She helps run the charity store next door, too."

"A charity store?" Fern asked.

Veronica nodded. "They're really serious about helping around here."

That made Fern look up. "I'd love to get involved with something like that."

"Yeah?"

Fern nodded. Her whole life had been about helping. Although Hank had abused her kind nature, she didn't want to lose that part of herself just because one person had treated her badly. She'd always been passionate about helping people, and if she could get involved with more things around here, she would be giving back to the community. Besides, it would help her meet new people around here and settle in. It was the only way she could imagine becoming a part of Waterstead rather than staying an outsider.

"You should head on down there sometime and talk to Linda, then. She'll be thrilled about the extra pair of hands, she can never get too much help. And she's such a kind woman." Veronica dusted her hands after going through one box. "I don't know how I would have settled in here without her."

"I'll be sure to stop in," Fern said. "It's such a nice little town, and everyone seems to be so welcoming and homey."

"And you'll fit right in," Veronica said with a smile. "You're different than the rest of the world."

Fern frowned, unsure if that was a compliment. Her stomach twisted into a knot. She knew she was different. She carried all kinds of baggage when others seemed to be carefree and able to move forward without the past tugging them back all the time. She'd worked for years, keeping a smile on her face and not letting anyone know she was struggling when things at home got particularly hard. She hated that her past showed enough that a stranger like Veronica could see through her mask on the first day.

"In what way?" Fern asked.

"You're a visionary," Veronica said in a breathy voice. "You see heaven in a grain of sand, beauty in a flower...that sort of thing. So many people see life for what it is, not what it can be. I'm excited to have you on board!"

Relaxing, Fern sighed in relief at the compliment. Veronica was a breath of fresh air, so different than the people Fern had been surrounded by. She made Fern feel at ease, her warm nature drawing Fern in.

"I have to go. I have a few things to take care of," Veronica said. "Here." She handed Fern a set of keys with a fluffy yellow keychain.

"You're giving me the keys already?" Fern asked, confused. "We haven't even signed any contracts, and I haven't put up a security deposit, first and last month's rent..."

"We'll figure that out later," Veronica said with a wave of her hand. "I know you're not going to pull one over on me. I can tell you're one of the good ones." She winked.

A thrill ran through Fern. She'd come to town just yesterday, and she was already in possession of a brand-new life.

"Thank you," she said, beaming. She didn't have the words to tell Veronica how grateful she was. It went so much deeper than just being glad she had a job and somewhere cozy —well, eventually cozy—to stay. This was about escaping Hank, her past, the demands, and the time she would never get back. Finally, she could start a life she could live on her own terms.

"You have my number," Veronica said. "Call me if you need anything. And do what you like with the place to really make it home, okay? I'm serious—no holds barred."

Fern nodded, and Veronica left with a flourish, leaving Fern behind in the studio apartment. Aside from a phone conversation after she'd sent in her resume, today was the first time Fern had communicated with Veronica. But she'd liked the woman right away—although she was a little strange—and she felt like they'd been friends for years.

Fern turned back to the apartment. She had a lot of work to do. She and Veronica had decided it would be best to start with the boxes and sort them into categories. That way, they could go through the most important things first and slowly take care of the rest. Fern would also sweep and dust—no small feat due to how old and dirty the place was. Then she would rearrange furniture, and finally move in.

First things first, Fern needed more light. The studio apartment had just as many large windows as downstairs to let in natural light, but most of them had curtains drawn over them, leaving the apartment in perpetual dusk.

Fern walked to the curtains and yanked them open. She coughed as dust puffed up in clouds, the particles dancing like glitter in the rays of sunshine falling through the windows. The window cast more light into the open-plan room, making Fern realize there was a lot more work to be done. More boxes and more dirt than she'd thought possible.

*Boxes can be cleared up and sorted out, and dirt can be cleaned,* she told herself. *Dirt is the simplest problem in the world, easy to solve.*

She grabbed a black bag from a roll of bags in the corner and collected what was clearly trash. The more she worked, kicking up dust, the dirtier she became, her fingers turning black from the grime. The apartment was hot, so she brushed her hair out of her face now and then, leaving streaks of dirt on her face and arms as she did. While she carried and stacked boxes, her clothes became just as dirty, with splotches of dirt and streaks of dust.

Fern didn't care. She was in her element. Working this hard for a good reason was always invigorating. Knowing she was going to reap the fruits of her labor, eventually living in the apartment she could only describe as fantastical, made everything worth the effort.

When she lifted a box in the corner, she disturbed a spider's nest. The large spider scurried toward Fern's feet, and she shrieked, jumping back. The spider kept coming, and she tapped her feet on the wooden floor to deter it. The moment she did, a plethora of little spiders fell off its back, the babies scattering now, too.

"Oh no!" Fern cried out.

She spotted a can of insect repellent and aimed it at the spiders, pressing down hard on the nozzle. But the can was as neglected as the rest of the apartment, and instead of releasing a steady stream of insect repellent toward the spiders—already thinning as they found corners to hide in—the can released a cloud of spray right into Fern's face.

She sputtered and coughed, suddenly unable to breathe. Her eyes burned with tears, and she stomped blindly in the direction of one of the windows. She tried to push it open, but it had been painted shut and her fingers couldn't get a good enough grip. She tried another window but to no avail.

The windows were all painted shut.

In her panic to get fresh air into her lungs, Fern rushed to the apartment door. Her burning eyes blurred the way, and she tripped over boxes, the trash bags tangling around her ankles, making her panic further. She finally reached the door and threw it open, running toward the outside door at the top of the stairs.

Suddenly, two men were in front of her, and she ran right into one of them. Large hands curled around her upper arms.

"Hey, now," a deep voice said.

Panic rocked Fern's body. She was suddenly back home, in her bed late at night, with Hank ranting about her mistakes, stomping up the stairs to scold her and punish her.

"I'm sorry!" she cried out, sobs racking her chest. "I'm so sorry!"

"Calm down, ma'am. Just breathe," the deep voice said, and it took a moment for Fern to realize she wasn't hearing Hank's spiteful growl.

She blinked her eyes open, wiping her tears. Through

narrowed eyes, she looked at the two men. One was tall and thin with dark graying hair and eyes the color of the sky. The other was almost as tall, with hazel eyes and sandy hair. They both looked worried but not like they were a threat.

"Oh," she said. "You're not..." A hiccup escaped her lips that turned into a laugh. "I was expecting someone else."

"This place is a dump," the first man said, letting go of her arms. "It's a wonder you expected anyone at all." He frowned at her.

"I didn't mean it that way," Fern said, a giggle escaping her again. When she was in a panicked situation, she often laughed. That reaction had gotten her into trouble more often than not. "I meant...never mind. It's complicated."

"It must be. What are you doing in my building?"

Fern blinked, trying to get rid of tears that just kept forming in her still-burning eyes. "I live here." The words tumbled out of her mouth before she could think twice about how it sounded.

The two men exchanged glances.

"Are you Thatcher?" Fern asked, putting two and two together.

"That's me," Thatcher said, nodding. He still looked confused. "It's clear you know who I am, but I still don't know who you are and why you're in my apartment."

Fern shook her head, as confused now as Thatcher and his friend. But the fresh air that blew in through the open door was a balm to her burning lungs, and her eyes started to clear. Her blurry vision subsided, and she had time to take in more of who she was looking at.

Thatcher was clearly a cowboy. It was written in the way he carried himself and the drawl with which he spoke.

The other man didn't look anything like a cowboy, but he was as handsome as anything. His hair was the color of beach sand, and his hazel eyes had flecks of gold. He was more muscular, too—a product of manual labor, Fern guessed. He didn't look like the type to spend his life in the gym to look good.

No, no, those muscles were all functional.

*Stop it, Fern! You can't ogle strangers and decide who they are. Not even handsome ones!*

Thatcher glanced past Fern at the boxes and dirt in the room she'd vacated.

"You live here, huh?" he asked, incredulous.

Fern looked over her shoulder and grinned. "It's not much, but it's home."

The men exchanged glances again. "I don't know what to make of this, Elliot. Do you?" Thatcher asked the younger man.

Elliot shook his head and held up his hands. "Hey, I'm just the contractor. But judging by the looks of her..." He glanced at Fern, and her stomach erupted in butterflies. No matter how much she scolded herself, she couldn't get rid of the feeling, and her cheeks reddened as she failed to contain herself.

Great. Now she not only looked like a squatter, she looked crazy, too.

"I don't know whether we should call the police or an ambulance," Elliot finally said.

Fern gasped. "Excuse me?! I don't need either, thank you very much! And I don't appreciate what you're insinuating."

"Now, now, calm down," Thatcher said. "No one's insinuating anything. But you are on private property, and we need to take care of this matter. Why don't we go downstairs, get a bit of fresh air and sunlight, and discuss this like adults?"

Fern nodded. Thatcher was right—that was the best way to handle it. She felt worked up after what Elliot had said. How dare he call her crazy! She'd grown up in a house where "crazy" was the order of the day, and one thing was for sure—Fern was many things, but *crazy* was not one of them.

When they stepped onto the grass in front of V Studios, Thatcher took out his phone and talked to someone. Elliot and Fern stood together in awkward silence.

"I'm Elliot," he said when the silence stretched thin and became almost unbearable.

Fern hadn't said anything until now—she hadn't wanted to talk to him. "Fern," she grumbled. "And I'm not crazy."

Elliot frowned at her. "Who said you were crazy?"

"What else would you want to call an ambulance for?" she demanded.

"In case you're hurt," Elliot said carefully. "You were coughing uncontrollably, and your eyes are still so red, although they're less watery now. I was just worried."

The fight in Fern died down a little, and she felt like an idiot for jumping to the "crazy" conclusion right away. Of course, an ambulance was for the injured, not just to cart away loonies. Even if the latter was mostly why an ambulance had come to Fern's house while growing up.

"I'm sorry," she muttered. "I just..." She sighed. How could she begin to explain what was going on in her head? She reacted to her past whenever something happened in the present. "I'm okay."

Elliot didn't look like he believed her, but that was his problem. Physically—and even mentally—she was fine. She didn't need any medical attention. Her emotional state was a different story. Aside from feeling mortified now that she'd put her foot in it, she was a mess. The past kept coming back in flashes. Hank, with his hands around her arms, shaking her so many times, she was too dizzy to stand. Her mother, saying all kinds of unintelligible things, blabbering on in gibberish to deal with the twisted mess their lives had become.

The ambulances arriving to take her mom away until her

episode passed.

And staying behind with Hank. Alone. If there was ever anything scarring in her life, being left behind with Hank was it.

If Fern had had a father in the picture, a man who'd cared enough not to leave his wife and daughter in the lurch, maybe she would have opted to live with him when her mother had moved in with Hank. But Fern's dad had left a long, long time ago, never to come back. And Fern and her mother hadn't had anywhere to turn but to Hank, who'd offered a roof over their heads, food in their bellies, and a life of so much control, Fern still often felt like she needed to gasp for air.

Elliot took out his phone and scrolled through it. He'd dismissed her.

She bristled at that, but if he wanted nothing to do with her, that was fine. She didn't want anything to do with him, either.

She took a few steps away from him toward the art studio, where Thatcher was still on the phone, talking in earnest. Would he let her go back in and look at the artwork again? Clear up the room that was to be her classroom at the back of the building? She could try, but she didn't want to look for any more trouble than she'd already caused. She would just wait for Thatcher to get off the phone, and then she would talk to him about what was going on.

She should have mentioned that Veronica had hired her the moment Thatcher asked her what she was doing in the apartment. That would have made things so much easier for everyone. But she'd been in distress, panicking at the insect repellent fumes—and at the past hammering at her door. She'd felt the need to defend herself, to stand fast on her place in the world. She'd built herself up to be so defensive, it was her first reaction.

She never needed to justify herself. That was the rule she'd made for herself a while ago, before moving to Waterstead. All her life, she'd had to justify herself, her decisions, and her actions to Hank, who had found fault no matter what she did. She'd had to break that cycle and get out of the rut where she felt the need to always explain herself.

The irony was that now—after she'd finally taught herself how to defend herself and demand her space in the world—was the one time a justification had been in order.

But that was fine. She would talk to Thatcher, and they would clear the whole thing up. Veronica had said she was dating Thatcher, so in a moment, they would all be up to speed and everything would be okay. Thatcher looked like a man who could be reasoned with. He had a kind face and gentle eyes, and he seemed as level-headed as they came.

Unlike Elliot, who jumped to conclusions and didn't have the common decency to make simple conversation with a woman.

She glared at him while he continued to scroll on his phone. She decided she didn't like him. It didn't matter who he was, why he was here, or what he thought of her. He'd mentioned he was just a contractor, so he didn't even matter.

And he certainly wouldn't matter to her. She didn't need more men to decide who she was and what her role was in life. She'd fled Houston for exactly that reason.

Thatcher was in her good books, and Elliot was in her bad books, and that was the end of it.

Even though Elliot was drop-dead gorgeous.

She forced herself to look away. Staring at him would just make matters worse, and the last thing she wanted was for him to catch her staring. That would give him an ego boost he clearly didn't need...or confirm his suspicions that she was crazy.

She focused on the studio instead, waiting impatiently for Thatcher to finish.

# Chapter 4
# Elliot

"Sorry to take up so much of your time," Thatcher said to Elliot once he got off the phone, approaching Elliot where he still stood on the lawn.

"Oh, not at all. I told you, I set aside the day. I'm in no rush."

"Please, look around and tell me what you think of the cabinets we discussed," Thatcher said.

Elliot nodded.

When he and Thatcher had pulled up to the studio, they'd met in front of the building, and Thatcher had explained his plan to Elliot. He wanted to fix the place up for his girlfriend so she could run her business from it.

Elliot was impressed that she was starting a business, too. They both seemed like dynamic people, and it always impressed Elliot when people took the initiative to make something of their lives and were willing to do the work.

"I'll have a look around," Elliot said, glancing at the insufferable woman again. She was downright strange, and it irked Elliot when people jumped to conclusions about his intentions. He didn't like people who went out of their way to make life harder for others, and clearly, she was out of line.

Even if she looked angelic, with her auburn hair and green eyes. When he'd first seen her, she'd nearly taken his breath away, even while she was covered in dirt and gasping for air.

But looks weren't everything, and he wasn't about to let a pretty face distract him.

He pushed the studio door open. The bell jingled above his head, announcing his presence to an empty room.

The studio was spacious, with incredible sunlight streaming in from the windows. Art pieces for sale had been installed on the walls in various displays. Elliot loved art, but nothing particularly caught his eye. He was a man of very specific tastes.

He walked to the office and studied the room, envisioning the cabinets and built-in desk Thatcher had asked for. He took a few measurements, which he captured on his phone before moving to the next room. This room would only get cubbies, like an artist's locker room. These narrow compartments would be tall and deep enough to store a variety of canvases and art kits.

Elliot had done work for all manner of homes and businesses, but he liked the idea of working here. He'd never helped create a space for artists to use. He was already thinking about paint storage in a cool, dark space in the corner. He also decided it would be good to add an electronic display for slides that could be used for inspiration.

While he worked, he heard steps on the stairs outside. A moment later, a muffled conversation between Thatcher and Fern sounded from above. Elliot didn't mean to eavesdrop, but he couldn't help but overhear. He couldn't make out the words they were saying, but the overall tone sounded friendly.

That was a relief. Their conversation had nothing to do with Elliot, but the last thing he wanted was to be involved with evicting a squatter. And to be fair, Fern had looked *a lot* like a squatter, covered in dirt and claiming that she lived in the mess upstairs.

After wrapping up their conversation, Thatcher and Fern walked down the stairs into the shop through the front door, whose bell jingled with their arrival.

"Ah, there you are," Thatcher said when Elliot stepped into the large art studio. "Everything is taken care of."

"Glad to hear it," Elliot said with a smile. He meant it, too.

"Veronica employed Fern this morning to work at the studio, and she's going to move into the apartment. That's what she was doing here." He chuckled. "Funny how things can look all bent out of shape for nothing, huh?"

"Right," Elliot said.

Fern smiled at him, and the smile shifted the constellation of freckles on her nose. Her face lit up, and she was even more beautiful than when she was hostile and feisty. She looked a lot more approachable now. The redness in her eyes was gone, too.

"I'm sorry for our rude start," she said. "I promise you, I'm not usually so hostile."

Elliot laughed, shuffling his weight from one foot to the other. "It's fine. These things happen." He still didn't know what to make of her. Now that she wasn't angry with him, attacking him, or making him think she was a little crazy, she was so much more attractive.

But he wasn't interested in getting involved with anyone, especially not a volatile woman like Fern. He was here to do a job, and after that, he would leave and start over somewhere else.

"I talked to Veronica, and—"

The bell above the door jingled again, and in walked a woman with shorter dark hair and large, soulful brown eyes.

"You're all here," she said with a smile. "Quite the adventure so soon into our journey, huh?"

Thatcher pecked Veronica on the mouth, and she smiled warmly at him, running her hand down his arm affectionately.

"Things will never be boring," Thatcher said to her.

"And I wouldn't have it any other way." She was still smiling when she turned her attention to Elliot. "I'm sorry, I'm Veronica Tellez. This is my studio, and Fern is, as of a few hours ago, my employee."

"Elliot Garner," Elliot said politely, shaking her hand. He didn't offer any comment about Fern. The whole thing seemed bizarre to him, but he got the feeling that Veronica and Thatcher were cut from the same cloth. They made decisions on impulse and largely followed their gut.

Elliot wasn't the type of man to do that. He was always calculated, working everything out to a tee. That way, he kept the number of surprises waiting for him to a minimum. He knew exactly what to expect and how to handle it.

But to each their own.

"The studio is just lovely," Elliot said. "With so much natural light, the place is inspiring. I'm excited about what we're going to do here."

"Me too," Fern said, her cheeks getting pink with excitement.

"What are we going to do here?" Veronica asked, confused.

Elliot frowned and glanced at Thatcher, who burst out laughing. "Oh! I didn't tell you. I called Elliot in to help me with a few renovations at the house—"

"A few?" Veronica asked skeptically, crinkling her nose. So, they were all aware that this was a very big project. Good.

"Yeah," Thatcher said pointedly. "And I asked him to take care of a few things here at the shop, too. You need a better office if you're going to run it like a business, and we can really make this a good place for you and your students-to-be."

"And Fern," Veronica added.

Elliot glanced at the woman. A small smile played on her lips, and her large green eyes sparkled with delight. She was happy to be here. And Veronica seemed happy to have her.

That look of delight on her face only made Fern all the more beautiful.

*The beautiful ones are usually the crazy ones*, Elliot told himself. *Steer clear of this one. It's better to just stay focused on the project at hand. It's always better because work can be trusted, and people can't. Especially not women.*

Fern's eyes locked on Elliot's, and his stomach twisted with a strange sense of yearning that told him his body hadn't gotten the memo his brain had just dished out.

"Well, then, it sounds like we're all on the same page," Veronica said. "Finally," she added with a laugh. "I'm excited about what's going on here, too!"

She smiled happily at Elliot, and he decided he liked Veronica and Thatcher very much. They were a little different from the people he'd had to deal with in his life, but they were kind and sweet and clearly very fond of each other. It was a strange concept to him that two people romantically involved with each other actually *liked* each other.

But Elliot supposed that was what happened when both people were committed to the relationship.

"Would you like to see what I had planned for the back room?" Elliot asked, wanting to show Veronica he was adept at his job.

Veronica nodded. "Show me. And Fern, too."

Elliot led the two women to the back room, Thatcher tagging along behind them. Elliot explained how he wanted to set up the cubbies for the students to store their things, the storage he had in mind for the paints and brushes, and how to approach the electrical needs of the space.

"I really like where you're going with this," Veronica said, clearly impressed.

Elliot warmed at her praise. Working with clients was so much more rewarding when they were on board with the job and believed in his skill and vision.

"What do you think, Fern?" he asked.

"I couldn't have thought it out better myself," Fern said, nodding.

Veronica nodded in agreement and looked at Elliot. "Fern is our new art teacher, so she'll be spending a lot of time in this room. Once it's ready and cleared out, of course..." She looked around at the piles of junk that covered every surface, including a large sleeper table that looked out of place.

"Oh, you're an artist, too?" Elliot asked Fern.

"Yeah, that's what I'm here for," Fern said with a smile.

Elliot had been under the impression that Fern would just run the store, but knowing she was an artist gave him a newfound respect for her. Elliot had always loved art, but he didn't have a creative bone in his body. He loved to explore art, read the emotions behind it, and get lost in the world the painter inhabited. Since he was a child, he'd always wished he had the ability to do something like that.

He'd resigned himself to the fact that his work was more physical and practical, and he'd accepted that he was good at what he did.

Everyone had a niche in life.

"Her work is really good," Veronica said, nudging Fern. Fern wanted to protest, but Veronica held up her hand. "You can't tell me it's not, because I'm hiring you specifically for the quality of your work. Own it, my friend."

Fern beamed at Veronica before she looked at Elliot. "Well,

there you have it. I'm good." She giggled and blushed, as if admitting she was worth her salt was somehow foreign to her.

"What kind of art do you do?" Elliot asked, curious now. Clearly, there was a lot more to Fern than met the eye.

"Oh, nothing as abstract and modern as what Veronica does," Fern said.

Elliot considered the paintings in the studio and nodded. All the paintings had vivid colors and large, abstract swishes of paint that melded together to convey a message of emotion.

"My work is a little more classic," Fern added.

"Which is why we are the perfect combination, covering all bases," Veronica said.

"Here, let me show you what I mean," Fern said, taking her phone out of her pocket. She flicked her fingers over the screen a few times before she turned it to face Elliot.

Elliot took it from her and paged through the images of paintings Fern had taken. The paintings were indeed more classic, but there was nothing generic about them. Fern seemed fascinated by people and landscapes. Elliot studied the art, looking at how she let the people she painted blend into the background as if they were swept away by their surroundings.

"This is incredible work!" Elliot exclaimed, forgetting to mute his tone. Art that swept him away was worth looking at. "Can I commission you for a piece of art, or do you only sell the pieces here at work?"

"Oh, sure," Fern replied. "I do work for clients as well. I can paint an array of things on demand. But I would need to sit down together and discuss what you have in mind. If you have somewhere in particular you want to display the art, I'd like to have a look at the space, too."

"That's interesting," Elliot said. No painter he'd talked to or artists he'd worked with had ever asked him where the painting would end up hanging.

"It's a little more hands-on," Fern admitted, "but the lighting in a room, the way the sun hits it, and the furniture and wall colors all affect how a painting comes to life. If there's a certain place for the painting, I like to make sure all the right nuances come to the foreground."

Elliot stared at Fern. She was clearly a dedicated artist and very good at her job. When she talked about her art, she sounded excited, and that excitement was contagious. Her passion for her work bubbled over, affecting Elliot, too.

"Well, we'll have to see how we can make a plan, then," he said to the woman who was becoming more interesting the more they talked.

"It's a process," Fern warned. "A commissioned piece of art isn't something that happens overnight. It takes time and patience, from all parties involved."

Elliot nodded. Patience was a virtue he happened to have in abundance, and the idea of spending that much time around Fern, with her passion so close to the surface, was enticing. She still confused him and irked him, but her artistic side, her love for her work, drew him to her like a magnet.

He wanted more of it. He felt like an addict who had taken one sip, and now he was hooked.

*Keep it together, man,* he told himself. *It's just about the art.*

"I told you she was good," Veronica said to Elliot and Thatcher.

Fern's cheeks colored lightly, and a smile spread across her face. She was beautiful when she smiled; Elliot wished she wouldn't stop. Something in him wanted to make her smile again so he could keep staring at her.

He cleared his throat and pushed the sensation away. He wasn't going to get *that* involved with Fern. All he would do was order a painting from her, something he could take with him when he left. Then they would go their separate ways.

"I have to get back to my errands," Veronica said.

"And I have some cleaning to do," Fern added. She looked at Elliot. "Let me know when you'd like to meet, and we'll discuss what you have in mind."

Elliot opened his mouth to answer, but Veronica chimed in. "We're going out to dinner tonight. Why don't you two join us?" She glanced at Thatcher, giving him a knowing look.

Thatcher nodded. "That sounds like a great idea. It will give you a chance to get to know the town you'll be working in for the foreseeable future."

Elliot hesitated.

"It will give us a chance to get to know each other, too," Veronica added. "And since we'll all be working together…"

Thatcher and Veronica were sold on the idea, and Elliot didn't want to be rude and turn them down. He would be working with Thatcher for a long time, judging by the amount of work he wanted done here and at the beach house. Elliot didn't want to decline and start off on the wrong foot. He could use the money, and he wanted to stick around Waterstead a little longer.

The town just drew him, and so did the people there. And even more now than before they'd arrived at the studio.

"I was planning to drive back to Rockport for some equipment," Elliot said. "But since we're not going to get to work right away, I'll just book my hotel."

"It will be good having you close at hand for the work," Thatcher said.

"We have an agreement to do this, then?" Elliot asked. They hadn't yet finalized the business part of his trip.

"Absolutely," Thatcher said. "I'll make sure the money is there as we move along. I want you to start here, and we'll tick things off as they cross our path."

Elliot grinned and held out his hand to Thatcher. Thatcher took it and smiled as they shook.

"It's going to be a pleasure doing business with you. I just know it," Thatcher said.

Elliot nodded, feeling the same way. He didn't know what it was about the small town that made him feel so at home, or what made these strangers already feel like family. And there was the captivating woman with the flaming hair and green eyes. He wasn't the type to close his eyes and jump, but he would do this job because he knew it was needed.

And he would take the rest as it came.

It was out of character for Elliot to jump into something without having all the paperwork in place, but Thatcher and Veronica were impulsive people. Their zest for life dragged Elliot with them like an undertow. Working in the midst of this creative explosion would be a treat. The town was a fresh change of pace to Elliot's typical day-to-day life, and he would get a great painting out of it, too. What more did a man like him need?

He glanced at Fern again, stopping himself before he came to an answer.

# Chapter 5
# Fern

After Elliot and Thatcher left, Veronica turned to Fern. "It's going to be fun tonight."

Fern smiled and nodded, although she wasn't sure if she felt as enthusiastic about it. She'd much rather spend her time in the studio, cleaning things up and getting ready to move in as soon as possible.

Elliot wanted to commission her for a job, and that was nice. She could use the money and loved to paint by commission. Those projects always offered a challenge. But she didn't want to go to dinner with Elliot. It felt a lot like a setup; a double date rather than just a dinner where everyone got to know each other.

Not that she would mention it to Veronica. The woman was already doing so much for her, and Fern was grateful she'd gotten the job, especially after making demands about a living space.

"Is everything taken care of with Thatcher?" Fern asked.

Veronica nodded and laughed. "He called me in a frenzy about you being here. He thought we picked up a squatter!

After I calmed him down, I explained to him what happened. We still talk past each other, you know?"

"Is it a new relationship?" Fern asked.

Veronica nodded. "It's one of those where we feel like we've known each other for years, but at the same time, we don't know anything about each other at all. We're still navigating the waters. All we know is that we belong together. The universe told us so."

"Oh, really?" Fern asked, intrigued. "That sounds big."

"It sounds like something from a movie," Veronica said with a giggle. "But it was impossible to get away from him, so we gave in, and it turns out we fit together like we've been made for each other. It's funny how that works. How you can find your person without knowing it."

Fern smiled and nodded, politely listening to what Veronica had to say. She was happy that her new friend and employer had found her happily ever after. In a way, Fern yearned for something like that to happen to her.

But it just wasn't in the stars for a person like her. She was convinced she drew everything that was complicated in the world to her. Some things like a warm, healthy relationship... they just didn't work out for her.

"Are you dating anyone?" Veronica suddenly asked, as if she could sense Fern's thoughts.

Fern shook her head. "No, I'm single. I don't want any distractions now, either. Not having any ties to Houston is what made it so easy for me to move here when the opportunity arose."

Veronica nodded. "It does make things easier when you don't have anything holding you back. But settling down and sprouting some roots is never a bad thing."

Fern agreed, but she still wasn't going to entertain the idea of settling down with someone else. She wanted to do it alone, though being single wasn't always her favorite status. Sometimes, Fern wished she had someone by her side who could understand her, who knew enough about her history that they could offer advice and support. And who encouraged her to live her dreams and chase her future with reckless abandon.

She'd thought she had that once, too. When she'd dated Derek, everything had felt like it was coming together for her. He'd been everything she'd wanted in a man—attractive, funny, smart, and wealthy to boot. Not that money mattered to her; she could build an empire with someone who shared her work ethic and hunger to improve her life.

Derek had turned out to be the wrong guy for her. Too many little things had crept in, changing who she was until finally, she didn't recognize herself. And when Derek had left her for another woman, the person he'd left behind was... different.

It was then and there that she'd decided to never change who she was for the sake of a man again. And if that meant she would be eternally single, that was fine. She'd rather that than lose herself again. She could lose a lot of things, but losing herself and her heart was not an option.

Which was why she was reluctant to go on this double date Veronica and Thatcher had arranged. Still, she could control the outcome of it. She was at the helm of her ship, and she would steer it whichever way she pleased.

"Do you have to leave right away?" Fern asked, changing the topic before Veronica could pry more into her personal life and the reasons for her relationship status. "I found a few extra things I want to show you."

"I have a bit of time," Veronica said with a smile. "Out here, we make our own schedules most of the time. It's liberating."

Fern smiled, liking the concept. She liked a lot about this

town, its people, and the promise of what her life could be here.

Veronica and Fern locked up the studio and walked up the stairs to the studio apartment. This was the route Fern would cover every day for the foreseeable future, and excitement filled her at the thought.

Once they were inside, Fern rehashed the story about the spiders in vivid detail. Now that the chaos had been averted—although the spiders were still in there somewhere—it was funny to look back on it. She told the story through thick laughter and giggles.

Veronica was also in stitches about it, laughing and giggling along with Fern. "I can't believe how these things happen! We'll have to get someone out to fumigate this place. I don't want to think about what other creepy crawlies live in these wooden floorboards and between the boxes."

Fern shuddered at the thought of more bugs in the apartment and promptly agreed to having the place fumigated before she moved in. The last thing she wanted was to share a home with all kinds of bugs that crawled over her while she slept.

"Look at this," Fern said, walking to a box she'd found in the far corner of the apartment after opening all the curtains. The box contained a whole bunch of old letters. The envelopes had yellowed over time, and the handwriting was loopy and intricate. The letters were tied together with a ribbon.

"Oh, this is a treasure," Veronica breathed, running her fingers over the letters. "It's such a shame to have to get rid of all of this."

"Is that what you want to do?" Fern asked with a frown.

Veronica nodded. "I don't know what else to do with them."

"I'd like to read them."

"That's your baby, then," Veronica said, shaking her head.

Fern gasped in surprise. "Don't you want to know who they were from and why someone kept them for so long?"

Veronica looked guilty. "I don't want to sound heartless, but I have a very complicated past that I'm trying to deal with. I've finally found my happiness, but for a long time, I was stuck in this black tar of depression that made it impossible to live, to even breathe. I've finally escaped that prison, and although it's still hard, I'm getting better. So I guess I just don't have what it takes to delve into someone else's past if I still don't have a handle on mine."

Fern nodded sympathetically. "I completely understand." Veronica's words made so much sense, but that didn't stop Fern from feeling curious. "Do you mind if I go through them and see what I find?"

"Not at all," Veronica said with a smile. "By all means, go on ahead. I just don't want to know, you know?"

"I know," Fern said, gently squeezing Veronica's hand to let her know she wasn't judging her in the slightest. Everyone had a difficult past, in one way or another, and they did what they needed to do to take care of it.

"I really have to go now," Veronica said. "I'll see you tonight, right?"

"Right," Fern said, trying to sound upbeat. "I'll go through some of this to get a jump on sorting it out, then head home to shower before I meet you. Where are we going?"

"The restaurant is called Fiddler. In a town this small, you can't miss it. It's opposite the pizza place, a block down from The Tequila Rose of Texas."

Fern giggled. "I'm sure I'll find it with that name as a landmark."

Veronica grinned. "We all refer to that place as our starting point, since it's so clear and no one misses it. The quirky name makes it a laugh, too. Everyone loves it. We'll meet at eight."

"I'll see you then," Fern promised, and Veronica waved goodbye before she left.

Fern was finally alone, and she took a deep breath and let it out slowly. She took out her phone and dialed her mom's number.

"*Cariña*," Mom said when she answered the phone. "I was hoping you would call." The Spanish lilt in her mother's voice made Fern's heart constrict. She'd only been away from home for two days, but she missed her mother so.

"How are you, *Mamá*?" Fern asked. "I miss you."

"I miss you so much, it hurts!" Rosita exclaimed. "Where are you?"

Fern wanted to tell her mother all about Waterstead and how incredible it was, but she stopped herself. She couldn't tell her mom where she was. If she did, Hank would find out and come after her. He would drag her back to Houston, kicking and screaming, letting her know every step of the way what a disappointment she was.

No, she couldn't share anything with her mother that might clue Hank in to where she was.

"I'm in a beautiful town by the water, *Mamá*," she said. "You would love it here, it's so beautiful. I found a job and a place to stay. You don't have to worry about me."

"I will always worry, Fernanda. You are my only one."

Fern smiled. "Thanks, *Mamá*. I'm safe, and I'm happy. How are you? How...are things at home?"

"You know Hank. He's always angry these days," Rosita said. "But it's not bad. He's upset you left. He'll want to know when you're coming back."

"We already talked about this," Fern said carefully. Hank's temper about anything she did was exactly why she'd left. "I'm not coming back. Not for good. I'm only coming to visit when I can. I need this, *Mamá*, you know that."

"I know, I know," Rosita said. "I just wish you understood how much I need *you*."

Fern closed her eyes, trying to interpret those words as an endearing compliment rather than a prison she couldn't escape. Her mother had to learn to stand on her own two feet; she was a grown woman. Fern couldn't be her pillar of strength for the rest of her life. Playing that role had eaten away at Fern, taking her away from the life she wanted to live.

"I'll call often," she said. "Remember, I always love you."

"*Te quiero,* Fernanda," Rosita said. "Call me soon."

"I will," Fern promised before ending the call.

Her heart was heavy after the line went dead. She wanted to be there for her mother—after all, what if something went wrong? What if she had another episode and Hank didn't bother helping her? Didn't give her the medication she needed or get her to a hospital?

But no. Fern couldn't always be the only adult in their family. Her mother and Hank were both grownups, and it was time they looked after themselves. Her mother had chosen to marry Hank, and Fern couldn't change that. She was tired of fighting a losing battle, and she had to look out for herself now. She'd given up too much of her life for her mother and Hank. It was time to put herself first and focus on what she needed.

No matter how hard that was.

She turned her attention back to the box of letters. She picked up a stack bound with a bronze ribbon. She unraveled the ribbon, spreading the letters across her lap after sitting down on the dusty floor.

The letters were all written by the same person, judging by the delicate handwriting—a woman, Fern guessed. The letters were also all addressed the same way. They merely had a date and "You" on the front.

The first letter in the pile dated all the way back to 1960.

*Dearest,*

*You told me this distance is for the best. You told me it would be better than the struggles we faced by trying to be together. I can't help but wonder if you knew what you were saying. You've always been so knowledgeable, so aware of how the bigger picture comes together. I've always trusted you, body, mind, and soul.*

*But I wonder if you were right about this. Because the distance is killing me. I ache for you every day, my love, and I can't see how any good can come from this kind of pain.*

*I hope in my absence, you'll find the answers you're looking for. I hope you'll overcome the obstacle that forced us apart. It causes me physical pain to be away from you, and I choose to believe that the pain is mutual. How can it not be when we are destined to be together? I know you feel the same deep love for me as I feel for you.*

*I will do what you asked of me, my darling. I will keep my distance, but know that it causes me great suffering, and I don't know for sure if we made the right choice.*

*Yours always,*
*M.*

Fern read the letter again, marveling at the precise handwriting and the eloquent words. The depth of the writer's sorrow made her ache. She wished she had a love burning as bright as this person's.

What had driven them apart? What had driven a wedge between them but hadn't ruined their love for one another?

Fern had to know. She opened the next letter, and the next, drinking in every word. The letters ranged from outpourings of emotion like the first one to letters of scolding and anger, where the writer demanded answers and to be given reprieve. Some of the letters were very vague, though it wasn't hard to discern the writer's emotional state in any of them. She expressed herself clearly.

When Fern squinted to read the words in the next letter, she realized she'd become so absorbed by the writer's delicate scrawl, she'd lost all track of time. It was getting so dark outside that the words were no longer legible.

And Fern would be late for dinner!

She tied the letters with the ribbon again, then put them back in the box before drawing the curtains. After locking up the apartment, she ran her hand over the door. This was home. She felt it already, even though she'd only been here for a day and the apartment was a long way from being lived in.

That didn't matter. Fern had fled Houston in search of a place she could call home, and it seemed she'd found it much quicker than she'd thought possible.

She climbed into her car and drove the short distance to the Airbnb where she had a lease for the next week. As she drove, she glanced at the shop names to find the restaurant. She spotted the bar Veronica had mentioned, smiling at the quirky name. She noted other places of interest—a convenience store, a laundromat, a salon.

The restaurant was impossible to miss, and once she knew where it was, she drove on to the Airbnb.

She would hop into the shower and wash off the grime she was covered in after a day of working in the dust. And then she would head out to the restaurant and get the double date out of the way.

She really wasn't in the mood for it. After a day on her feet, and her mind continually wandering back to the letters, she'd rather take a long hot bath and get into bed with a good book. Or sketch out some painting ideas floating around in her mind.

She would have to do that another time. She had people to impress, and she would do all she could to secure the job of a lifetime in a town that would become her home if she played her cards right.

Besides, seeing Elliot again was for business purposes. Even if she found him rude and a little pompous, something good could still come of it.

And Fern was a firm believer in allowing the good to prevail. There were silver linings everywhere if she just looked for them.

# Chapter 6
# Elliot

"I'm so glad you decided to stay in town and join us," Veronica said when Elliot arrived at the restaurant. Fiddler was a typical mom-and-pop restaurant, with its homey décor and a play area for children.

"You'll enjoy staying in town, I'm sure," Thatcher added.

A hostess took them to a table for four. Fern had yet to show her face, and Elliot frowned upon tardiness. But then, she'd looked reluctant about the evening, and Elliot had to admit he hadn't exactly wanted to accept the dinner invitation, either. But he felt obliged to be here, so he sat down at the table with the odd couple, smiling and nodding at all the right times as Thatcher and Veronica gushed about Waterstead and what a nice place it was.

Elliot had to agree with them on that front. The town was a picturesque little place, and something about it drew him in. The moment he'd driven into the town, he'd had the strange sensation of coming to a second home. It was the only reason he'd let himself be convinced to stay for a social evening.

"I'm sure you meet a lot of interesting characters in your

line of work, Elliot," Veronica said, flipping her dark hair over her shoulder.

"Oh, very," Elliot answered. "But I imagine any work that involves contact with clients can be interesting."

"Oh, you've got that right," Veronica said with a grin. "Add a dash of crazy to that statement, and you define most artists." She looked at Thatcher with a sparkle in her eye, and he grinned and squeezed her hand.

"I think you should call yourself eccentric instead," Thatcher said.

"Who said I was talking about myself?" Veronica asked, feigning shock.

Thatcher laughed. "Well, I just assumed—"

"You see, you should never assume what a woman is thinking," Veronica teased. "That can just get you in a whole bunch of trouble you're not ready for."

Thatcher laughed, holding up his hands in defense. "If there's one thing I learned," he said to Elliot, "it's that the woman is always right. Even when you don't think she is, she probably is."

"And here they say men aren't all that smart," Veronica said.

Elliot watched the couple banter back and forth, keeping the conversation rolling with little input from Elliot. Though he hadn't been in the mood for the evening, watching them now was entertaining. They were like an old married couple—two people who knew each other so well, everything about them was in harmony.

It reminded him of how his parents were together—so used to each other's company, they didn't know why they were apart. At least...that was how they used to be with each other. That ship had sailed a long time ago, and now awkward silences and tension replaced any conversation between them.

He shook off the thoughts, refusing to think about his parents' doomed relationship.

He focused on Veronica and Thatcher. He liked them and hoped that their relationship would stand the test of time. His parents hadn't managed that, and that was a shame. But Thatcher and Veronica had something special. It was the kind of relationship Elliot hoped he could have one day, but he doubted he would ever get that far. After all, he wasn't a people person, and it was infinitely harder to meet someone when he only got out for work.

He wouldn't be good company if he ended up on a date of some kind, anyway. Even the idea of this dinner was exhausting. Elliot was a lone wolf and liked to keep things that way. No one understood him, and he'd made his peace with that.

"How long have you two been together?" Elliot asked, trying not to seem rude by staying silent while Veronica and Thatcher joked with each other.

"Oh, not very long," Veronica said, glancing at Thatcher. "Just a few months."

"Really?" Elliot asked. That answer was almost impossible to believe. "You are so comfortable around each other."

Veronica shrugged. "Sometimes, fate just seems to know who to throw together. I wouldn't have been able to make a better choice myself." She smiled sweetly at Thatcher.

"And anyone who knows me knows that I can be a right pain in the neck if I want to," Thatcher added. "So it had to have been a great destiny that threw us together."

Veronica laughed softly. "You? A pain in the neck? I don't know where you get it from..." She offered him a mischievous look before facing Elliot again. "When we met, I was the one who was the pain, believe me."

Elliot shook his head. "I can't see how that could have been."

Veronica launched into the story of how she and Thatcher had met over a broken-down car, apple pie, and a dog who seemed to decide for them where he wanted them to be. It was a sweet story, though Elliot hadn't asked for all the details.

In his opinion, they talked a little too much. At least they were entertaining.

"I wonder what's keeping Fern," Veronica said, glancing at a dainty wristwatch.

"Maybe something came up," Thatcher offered.

"Or she's perpetually late...but she was on time this morning," Veronica mused. "I don't know her at all, so I don't know if this is normal. Should we worry?"

"I don't think we should worry just yet," Thatcher said gently. "Not much can go unnoticed in a town like Waterstead, so if something's wrong, I'm sure we'll hear about it in no time at all. And there will always be someone around to help."

"You're right. It's nothing like a deserted highway, huh?" Veronica fluttered her eyes at Thatcher, who laughed.

Elliot fought the urge to roll his eyes at how cliché these two were being. He couldn't deny that he enjoyed their company, though. As much as he liked being alone, there was something pleasant about Veronica and Thatcher and the way they were with each other. Elliot didn't feel the need to run away just yet.

It was a pity Fern wasn't coming. Although maybe she was wise to skip out on this dinner. It seemed an awful lot like a double date, and the last thing Elliot needed was for someone to set him up. He was happy on his own, running his business, going out on errands, not answering to anyone but himself.

Still, he would have liked to spend a bit more time with Fern and get to know her. She seemed quirky and interesting. But he didn't want Veronica and Thatcher to push them into something he might not want. He hated it when someone decided who he should be spending time with. That automatically set him against the idea.

Besides, he was leaving soon. Getting involved with anyone would be a mistake. Despite the town's homeyness, he had to remind himself none of this was permanent.

It was probably better that Fern was a no-show.

"Ah, here she is now," Veronica said.

*Well, so much for that idea,* Elliot thought.

Veronica and Thatcher stood, and Fern joined their party. When she walked to the table, Elliot could only stare.

She looked nothing like the creature covered in grime they'd found at the studio. Her skin was pale and unblemished, and her green eyes sparkled when she greeted them, hugging Veronica as if they were old friends. She wore the proverbial little black dress with ballerina flats to dress it down. Her auburn hair hung over her shoulders in loose curls.

When she turned to Elliot, her smile shifted the constellation of freckles on her nose. It was impossible not to stare at her, and Elliot had to force himself to look away.

"I'm sorry I'm late," she said. "I got caught up with those letters at the studio apartment and lost all track of time."

"We're just glad you could make it," Thatcher said.

When she turned to face Thatcher, she brushed against Elliot.

"Oh, sorry," she said to him.

Elliot shook his head and gestured to the open chair next to him. Veronica and Thatcher had strategically chosen their seats on the other side of the table so that Elliot and Fern would wind up next to each other.

It was all a part of their plan, he was sure.

"Here," Elliot said to Fern. "Have a seat." He pulled the chair out for her. There was no reason not to be a gentleman, and his mind was fuzzy now that she was here. She looked spectacular.

*Keep it together, man,* he told himself. *This is the same crazy woman from earlier, making demands and claiming a spot that wasn't even hers.*

But now that he was with her and she looked the way she did, it was harder to see her as a nuisance. She was beautiful, and her smile came easily. Elliot liked a woman who could smile and take anything in her stride. Life could be tough, and the last thing he wanted was a damsel in distress.

When Fern stepped around Elliot to get to her chair, she lost her balance while avoiding other diners, bumping into Elliot again. She turned to sit down, and her giant purse knocked against him.

"Oh," he said, taking a step back. "Are you trying to kill me?"

She blushed hard, and the flush in her cheeks only made her that much prettier, bringing out her eyes even more.

"Sorry, sorry. I'm all thumbs today," Fern muttered. She sat down and glanced at Elliot.

"Clumsy, huh?" he asked, a little frustrated.

"I can be sometimes," she said with a shy smile. "I've always been clumsy, and Hank would yell at me, telling me to be more careful, but you can't unlearn something like that, right? It's a personality thing. I've learned to just roll with the punches now."

"It's always better to accept who you are and learn to love your flaws," Elliot said.

"You think I'm flawed?" Fern asked.

"Oh, no, no. That's not what I'm trying to..." When she grinned at him, Elliot realized she was teasing him.

"My clumsiness gets me in all kinds of trouble, you know," Fern set, putting her giant purse on the floor between the two chairs. "Like today, for instance, I ended up with insect repellant in my eyes and mouth."

Thatcher and Veronica laughed, and when Fern didn't

seem bothered by their reaction, Elliot joined in. He had to admit, the way they'd met was funny. Bizarre, actually.

He still wasn't sure what to make of Fern. She was unpredictable, and that made Elliot uncomfortable. He liked to know what was going to follow. He liked being able to read people.

He couldn't get a read on Fern at all, and that frustrated him. What frustrated him more was that he desperately wanted to know what she was thinking.

Why did it even matter?

A server appeared and took their orders. Elliot noticed that Fern ordered pasta instead of a salad. He admired women who were comfortable enough in their skin to not be self-conscious and restrict themselves to diet drinks and salad. And Fern had every reason to be confident. She wasn't only beautiful; she carried herself with elegance and grace—when she wasn't throwing herself against doors in a desperate attempt to get fresh air, or making snappy remarks because she'd jumped to conclusions that were completely off the mark.

After the server disappeared with an order of pasta and pizza for the table, Fern turned back to Elliot.

"What letters did you get lost in?" Elliot asked.

"I found a box of old letters in the studio apartment, written by a woman a long time ago. They're so melancholic to read, and I feel so bad for her. Even though she might not even be alive anymore."

Fern recounted the letters and what was in them to the group. She spoke with nostalgia and emotion, and Elliot was starting to see that Fern approached everything with emotion. Maybe it was an artist thing. Nonetheless, it was beautiful to hear her talk, and he was intrigued by the story.

"I wonder if the writer could be found somehow," he said.

"There's nothing to go by," Fern said, shaking her head. "Not even a name."

"What about a handwriting specialist? Or fingerprints..." Elliot chuckled when he realized how ridiculous those ideas sounded.

"What bugs me more is that I don't know what the replies to those letters were," Fern said. "Or if there were any replies at all. It seems like a doomed relationship to me."

"Oh, that is unsatisfying!" Veronica cried out.

"I know," Fern said, nodding. "I didn't get through all of them—if I hadn't looked at the time, I would still be sitting there, reading in the dark! Hopefully, there will be an answer somewhere in there to heal my weak heart." She giggled and turned her bright green eyes to Elliot. He cleared his throat and looked away, lest he should fall into those eyes.

*Keep your head on straight. Don't think about what could be. You're here with a plan, and you're leaving soon. Just because she gets emotional about other people's love stories doesn't mean anything.*

"Did you grow up in Rockport?" Fern asked Elliot, as if she knew he was trying to keep it together. The change of topic was a relief.

"Almost. I grew up in Chicago. My parents moved out here when I was much younger. They wanted to break away and find a place on the coast. I guess most of my life is around here, but I'll be leaving soon."

"Leaving?" Veronica and Fern asked in unison.

"Where?" Fern added.

"Why?" Veronica demanded.

Elliot swallowed hard, feeling like he was suddenly under an inquisition.

"I want to be able to grow my business, and I feel I've hit a limit. I'm stuck out here. I want to go back to a city and see what life can bring me there. Sometimes, it's good to start over."

Fern nodded. "I admire someone who can pick themselves up and start over."

"I think everyone at this table has done that," Veronica said. She poured out a glass of water from the pitcher on the table and lifted it in salute.

"I don't know how you could want to move *away* from the coast," Fern said, swirling the water in her own glass. "Being here is so liberating. Coming here from the big city was a lot more freeing than I realized. Being at the coast just makes me feel alive."

There it was—the passion Elliot saw peeking through every now and then. When Fern talked like this, it made him wonder what it would be like to kiss her.

*Now you really must get a grip,* he scolded himself. He couldn't think that way about her.

"I think a fresh start is a fresh start, whichever way it goes," Thatcher defended Elliot. Elliot was glad someone was on his side.

Elliot had known Veronica and Thatcher had both uprooted themselves and started over in Waterstead. He hadn't known Fern had done the same.

"Where are you from?" he asked her.

"Houston," she said.

"And you don't miss home?"

She shook her head. "Home is relative." She sniffed, looking uncomfortable. Elliot watched her shut down a little, her smile fading, her eyes dulling. Whatever was back there in Houston, it wasn't pleasant for her to think about. He didn't want to be the reason she looked like the light had gone out of her, so he changed the topic.

"Why do you like painting people so much?" he asked.

"Oh." Her eyes brightened again, the spark returning. When that spark twinkled in her eyes, she was incredibly beautiful—an inner beauty like hers was rare. "People say so much without using words. Did you know that only seven percent of communication is verbal? The rest lies in body language, in micro-expressions, in the way we approach the world. When I paint, I want to capture that. It's like writing, but without words."

She explained to Elliot, Thatcher, and Veronica how she'd always thought art was a form of communication all on its own. Veronica nodded, understanding a great deal more about what art meant than Thatcher or Elliot did. She was an artist, too, after all.

"You see," Veronica said to Fern, "what you do is so much different than what I do, and we use the same medium. I aspire to evoke emotion in the viewer with the colors I use. You evoke emotion in the way you portray people."

"And landscape, the way it comes to life and draws you in," Fern said. "It's exciting to think about how different our approaches can be when we're doing the same thing."

She and Veronica smiled at each other, sharing a glimpse into a secret world that the rest of them would never understand. Elliot felt a pang of jealousy that they saw something he would never see. He envied the reckless abandon with which the two women—Fern, especially—seemed to dream.

Fern glanced at him again, her face bright with the light that shone within her.

Elliot wanted to be closer to Fern. He wanted to touch her, feel her soft skin under his fingertips.

*What is wrong with me? I've never been interested in anyone, and suddenly my emotions are so powerful, I don't know what to do with myself.*

It had to be the strangeness of the day, he decided. That, and the way the small town seemed to hypnotize anyone who drove into it. Waterstead made Elliot feel like he was in an alternate reality. The kind of place where fairytales might just come true.

*Don't be ridiculous. It's just these two women talking about how they look at the world through different eyes that's making me think this way. I'm not an artist, but hearing them talk the way they do, I can almost envision things the way they see them, and that's what's sweeping me away. I'm in the undertow of dreamers and artists, and that's not who I am. I'm logical and down-to-earth. I see things the way they are and not the way they might be.*

Elliot had been through his fair share of difficulties. He'd watched the love between his parents slowly fade away until nothing was left. He'd seen how they'd hoped for a future together, only to grow apart so much that they were barely amicable.

To watch love die like that between two people had hurt him. It had killed his hope for the fairytale love he had thought he would one day find, and it had made him look at life through a lens of realism. And it was better that way—as long as Elliot knew how to manage his expectations, he would never be hurt and never be disappointed.

It wasn't that he didn't want a happy ending. He just understood that it wasn't as easy as some people made it seem.

Women like Fern were dangerous. She believed in something that didn't exist, and she was so passionate, she threatened to sweep Elliot into her dream world. He just had to keep his head about him, think logically, and remember that not everything could be seen through rose-colored lenses.

Was he cynical? Not at all. He was just realistic about what to expect from life and what he could achieve.

When Fern smiled at Elliot again, he pushed away his feelings of attraction. He offered a smile in return, proud of himself that this time, his heart didn't skip a beat and he didn't wonder what she was thinking.

The food arrived, and they ate while making conversation. Veronica and Thatcher laughed and chatted, Fern shared her views, and the evening was downright pleasant. The conversation remained shallow, though, scratching the surface of who they were and what they did.

By the time the evening was over, they'd all eaten a little too much, and Elliot was glad to say goodnight and make his way back to the hotel room he'd booked. He liked spending time with Fern a little too much. It would be good to get away from her and clear his mind.

He would probably be in town for a while to take care of the work Thatcher needed. But he would keep a clear mind, tomorrow, everything would look different. He'd just been swept up by everything that had happened during the day.

Tomorrow would be better, where Elliot would go about business as usual and look at things objectively.

"Thank you for joining us tonight," Veronica said to him as they said their goodbyes. "I hope you enjoyed yourself."

"I did," Elliot said. He glanced at Fern.

"I'm sure we'll all be seeing more of each other," Thatcher said.

Elliot nodded. "We'll get started first thing in the morning."

"Looking forward to it," Thatcher said.

Fern walked to Elliot and held out her hand. He shook it, noticing how soft her hands were.

"I'm sure I'll see you around sometime soon," she said with a smile.

Elliot caught himself before he blurted out, "Looking forward to it." He cleared his throat. "I'm sure we will," he said instead.

"Sweet dreams," Fern said.

Elliot offered her a smile before turning his back on the party and walking across the street toward the hotel. He needed to get some sleep and clear his mind so that tomorrow morning, he could start afresh and focus on the job at hand. He wasn't going to let someone like Fern and the passionate way she looked at the world distract him from what he'd come here to do.

His business was what mattered right now, the future where he would start life anew in a city far from here. He didn't have time to explore other views and other ways of thinking.

He didn't have time to explore what he could feel for Fern. He wasn't here for anything like that. He was on his way out, one foot already out the door.

He just had to keep reminding himself of that.

# Chapter 7
# Fern

The next day, Fern arrived at V Studios bright and early and ready to work.

"Oh, I'm glad you're early," Veronica said, offering Fern a quick hug. "I'm on my way out."

"Out?" Fern asked.

"Yeah. It's last minute, I know, and I'm leaving you alone on your first day, but it can't be helped. Del Mar College in Corpus Christi asked me to teach a workshop."

"Oh, that's big!" Fern exclaimed.

"I know," Veronica said gleefully. "I'm hoping the exposure will help us with students in the long run."

"Of course, you go do your thing! Represent us. I'm sure it will be a blast."

"I hope so," Veronica said brightly, though she looked a little nervous.

"You're going to nail it. You'll do just fine," Fern reassured her.

"I'm holding all my thumbs this works out right. I've barely had time to prepare! But that's when the creativity really flows, right? Are you going to be okay here?"

Fern nodded. "I can figure it out. If I get stuck, I'll send you a text or call Thatcher."

"He might not know what to do. He's not much of an artist," Veronica said, glancing around the gallery that made up the front room of the studio. "I guess it's you and me both in the deep end today."

Fern squared her shoulders. "We can do this. We are great artists, and we know what we're doing."

"That's right," Veronica said. She still looked a little nervous, but Fern had faith that they would both figure it out.

"I drew up a list of things for you to take care of as soon as you get a chance today." Veronica handed Fern a handwritten list.

Fern glanced at the list. It covered quite a few things, including sorting out the gallery, taking care of the back room to start a classroom, and making sure the custom pieces for customers were ready for them when they came to pick them up. Veronica explained that all the pieces had already been labeled and packaged in the office, so Fern couldn't get that wrong.

Finally, Veronica took her leave, and Fern was left alone. She took a deep breath and let it out slowly.

"This is going to be easy," she said out loud, trying to convince herself. "It's just a couple of tasks and a few people to meet, and I'm good at all those things. This is good."

It was what she'd wanted for a long, long time, after all. Fern had wanted to make a career out of her art and not just use it as an escape. It was almost poetic that she'd escaped so she could create her art, and here she was, in a position where she could finally make her dreams come true.

Throughout her life, Fern had sacrificed so much. She would have loved to study at a college like Del Mar, to learn the tricks of the trade, to study under the greats and become an artist whose name spread far and wide.

None of those things had happened. Aside from the money that just hadn't been there, she'd stayed to protect her mother from Hank. And to protect her mother from herself.

It had been liberating when she'd finally decided to leave and let her mother deal with her life by herself. Her mother was old enough to make her own decisions. Rosita had episodes from time to time, but she still knew what was good for her and what wasn't. She could make clear-minded decisions.

The fact that all of Rosita's decisions had been bad wasn't Fern's fault. Heaven knew she'd tried everything to convince her mother to take a new direction. Since her mother hadn't wanted to learn, it'd been up to Fern to look after herself.

And that was what she was doing here in Waterstead. She'd finally put herself first and was only looking out for one person now: Fern.

Shortly after nine, the door jingled.

"Hi! Welcome to V Studios," she said to the younger couple who walked through the door. "How can I help you?"

"We're here to pick up a custom piece for Tom Felton," the man said.

"Of course, I'll be right back," Fern said, hurrying to the office. She found the painting with "Tom Felton" on the label and carried it back to the gallery.

"We're so excited about this!" the woman cried out at seeing the painting.

"You made a great choice coming to V Studios for your art," Fern said warmly. "We hope to see you again soon."

"Oh, absolutely," they said in unison, and Fern smiled.

They left the studio, and Fern felt a sense of accomplishment. She hadn't done anything to create the piece for them, and giving them the art hadn't exactly been a big hurdle, but she felt like she was a part of something bigger. It felt good to see people light up and get excited about the art they'd ordered.

She glanced around the gallery. Veronica had put up her abstract pieces, some of them on the walls and some of them on pedestals around the room. Other paintings filled the walls, too—paintings created by Veronica's clients. The pieces were great in their own right, but the way they were displayed... something felt off.

Fern frowned and tilted her head. She closed one eye and tried to figure out what she was seeing.

It was the color scheme, she realized. The walls were white, and the abstract paintings had beautiful pops of color. However, some of the colors clashed, taking away from the paintings rather than bringing something to the room that begged for a buyer's attention.

She walked from one room to the other, studying each painting and all the colors Veronica had used. Finally, she started taking the pictures down from the walls and putting them on the floor. Bit by bit, she rearranged the paintings. She worked along the color wheel, going from red to orange to yellow, followed by green and blue, pink and purple, and ending with the grayscale images.

When she was done, she stepped back to admire her handiwork.

"This is good," she said to herself. "Much better. I even want to buy some of these."

She smiled, pleased with herself. When Veronica came back, Fern would explain how she'd played with the color schemes. Each painting offered an emotional trip for the viewer, but in a collection, they had to work together to make them that much more compelling. Fern knew a little about displays and marketing, and how applying the principles of what drew customers made all the difference.

She'd set a few paintings aside that didn't work with the

way she wanted to put them up, deciding to use them in the window display.

Art was, after all, about position as much as it was about depiction.

Fern climbed into the window display and started to arrange the paintings against pedestals and fabrics that accentuated the colors. She had a couple of pins between her lips, wrapping the fabric around the pedestals holding the paintings, when an older woman waved at her from the street. Fern waved back, and the woman opened the door to the studio.

"I'll be right with you," Fern called out, sticking two more pins into the fabric to be sure it held.

The display was beautiful and would do exactly what she intended—it would draw the eye and make passersby wonder what else was inside.

"Sorry about that," Fern said to the woman with a smile when she stepped back into the gallery.

"Are you new?" the woman asked. "Veronica mentioned she wanted to employ someone and expand. I didn't realize she was already this far. I'm Linda."

"Oh! It's my first day here. I'm Fern." Veronica had mentioned Linda, and Fern was pleased to meet her.

"I think the whole thing is just grand," Linda said, looking around the gallery. "When Veronica arrived in Waterstead, she didn't know what she wanted to do. Thatcher bought her this studio, and it was the best thing that could have happened to her—well, the studio and the man who dotes on her so much. I live down the beach from them, and I've seen them around since the day they arrived."

Fern nodded. "They're a great couple, and the studio has a lot of potential."

"You bet," Linda said. "Are you an artist, too?"

Fern nodded and explained how she approached art, how

her work was so different from what Veronica and several of her clients did.

"It's always good to branch out and expand horizons," Linda said. "Waterstead is the kind of town that asks for it, you know. People around here think they come to Waterstead to settle, but their world changes completely, and it's not about settling down as much as spreading their wings to fly."

"That's very poetic," Fern said. She didn't add that it was exactly what she was doing here, too.

"Your window display is just beautiful," Linda said. "I think you have an eye for color and art. Even the gallery looks incredible."

"Did you see it before?" Fern asked.

"Oh, since the moment the studio opened. I'm very invested in Veronica's journey. She deserves a happy ending after everything she's been through."

Fern wanted to ask what Linda was talking about but didn't want to pry into Veronica's life. She wasn't the type to gossip about someone. Waterstead was a small town where everyone was in everyone's business, as far as she could tell, but that didn't mean she had to be that way. She was a city girl. If Veronica had something to share, Fern knew she would confide in her when the time was right.

She had her own secrets, too.

"Would you like to take a look around and see if something catches your eye?" Fern asked.

"Oh, I'm here to pick up a commissioned piece," Linda said.

"Of course!" Fern had seen Linda's name on the other painting in the office but hadn't put two and two together. "I'll be right back."

She retrieved the painting and returned to the gallery. Linda was studying one of the smaller paintings, her head tilted. She looked emotional.

"I think I'll take another, after all," Linda said, gesturing to the painting. "This one really speaks to me."

It was a painting created by one of Veronica's clients, a landscape of the beach with stormy clouds in the sky. The painter had managed to create a sense of urgency behind the pending storm.

"It's a great choice," Fern said. "I always admire painters who can bring a landscape to life with this much emotion."

Linda nodded. "That's exactly why I love art so much. It's a communication between two people who have never seen each other and perhaps never will. I love the idea that somehow, despite being isolated sometimes, we're never truly alone. There are others who experience the same things we do, and a painting like this drives that message home."

Fern nodded. She liked Linda a lot. She was outspoken and didn't bother talking about the weather or the news. She jumped right into deep conversation with tidbits of wisdom.

"Let me ring this up for you," Fern said, walking around the counter. She wrote down the details of the painting Linda had bought along with the one she'd ordered.

"Would you like me to package that for you?" Fern asked. "I think we have bubble wrap and packaging in the back."

"Don't worry, I'll set it up against this one in my car. It's not far to my home on the beach."

"Before you go, I'd like to ask you something. Veronica mentioned you are involved with a charity?"

"Oh, yes," Linda said, her eyes lighting up.

"I'm looking to get involved with something like that. I—"

"You're more than welcome to come over when you have a chance, and we can see what you'd like to do. I have all kinds of projects going." Linda smiled, looking excited. "I'm sure I can find a space for you, and something that gets you excited and passionate."

That sounded like a good idea to Fern—she was all about

passion. Without it, nothing felt worth doing, and she'd been stagnant for so long, putting everything in her life aside for someone else. It was time to do things that mattered to her, things that made her happy. She'd always wanted to help people, and if she could get involved here, she could do some good on top of carving out a new life for herself.

"That would be amazing," Fern said, nodding.

"Come by after work sometime when you have a chance, and I'll show you around."

Fern agreed and thanked Linda before the older woman went on her way. She felt another sense of accomplishment after Linda left. Not only was she managing her first workday without Veronica, but she was getting involved in more projects and meeting more people around town. If she kept going like this, she would feel at home and settled in no time.

Feeling pleased with herself, Fern walked to the back room, where more paintings were stored. She chose one to put up in the now-vacant place to make the gallery complete once again.

For a while, Fern did a bit of admin behind the counter, manning the gallery while she completed the tasks on Veronica's list. The gallery became quiet. A few people passed the windows, pausing to study the window display before walking on. Though they hadn't ventured inside, Fern liked that they stopped to take in what she'd done with the display.

Finally, after she'd completed the tasks on the list, she walked into the back room and planted her hands on her hips. The room would be a classroom, but a lot had to be done to convert it. Elliot would install cubbies for the artists after taking care of the other jobs Thatcher had for him, but to have space to install the cubbies, the room had to be cleared out. Right now, a large sleeper table dominated much of the room, and boxes and blank canvases were stacked against the walls. The room was nothing more than a storage space.

Fern wanted to clear it as soon as possible. The quicker they could convert the room into a classroom, the quicker she could have students to teach and build the business into something more than just a gallery.

Veronica was such a sweet person, and although this position had started off as just a job to Fern, a way to escape and start over, she was dedicated now to making it work even better than Veronica envisioned. Fern was allowed to breathe here, to live without looking over her shoulder all the time and apologizing for everything she did. She wanted to live life to the fullest now that she had the chance.

She got to work. It took heavy lifting to get the boxes out of the way and move the canvases to a storage space in the office. Right now, the space was for commissioned work, so she lined up the paintings alongside the blank canvases for the time being. She would bring them back to the room eventually, but she needed space to move.

The first order of business, now that the space had been cleared out a bit, was to move the large table. She gripped the tabletop with two hands and tried to pull, but the heavy table wouldn't budge. She tried to get around it and push it aside, putting all her weight behind it, but it still didn't move. She scratched her head, trying to think of a way to move it. She wasn't very strong, but she was smart.

After thinking for a moment, she walked to her car and took out the length of rope she always kept in her trunk. With the rope slung over her shoulder, she returned to the classroom and tied it around two table legs. She wrapped another loop around her waist and leaned forward against it, hoping that her weight, gravity, and the rope would move the table.

For a moment, the table scraped across the floor, and it looked like it was working. But then Fern's feet slipped on the wooden flooring. Her legs shot backward, and because the rope kept her body in place, she fell flat on her face.

A chuckle sounded behind her, and Fern jerked her head to look over her shoulder, her hair tumbling into her face. She pushed it aside and huffed.

Elliot leaned against the doorpost, his arms folded across his chest and his eyes glinting with amusement. "Well, that's one way to do it," he remarked.

She rolled her eyes, embarrassed and frustrated. "If you're not going to help, leave the room."

"You don't look like you need help. You're doing so well."

She got up and rubbed her knee where she'd hit the wooden floor. It might leave a bruise, but it was nothing compared to her humiliation that Elliot had found her face-down on the floor.

"What are you doing here?" Fern asked.

"I'm here to measure for the cubbies. Although, I could have robbed you blind and you wouldn't have known."

Fern blanched. She hadn't heard the bell above the door jingle to announce Elliot's arrival.

"I wasn't here that long," she said. "And I'm making myself useful, which is a lot more than you're doing."

Elliot chuckled again and shook his head. His smirk was infuriating, and it was even more frustrating that he looked so good leaning against the doorpost like that. Not to mention that smile on his handsome face, his hazel eyes dancing with laughter.

"Can I help you?" he asked.

"Help me make a space for the work you're supposed to be doing in here? Sure."

"Are you always this snappy, or do I get special treatment?"

She glared at him. Despite her shortness with him, he still

had a smirk on his face, and it was a lot more handsome than she wanted to admit.

For a moment, they faced off. Since Fern's arrival, everything had been so bizarre, especially when she and Elliot were in the same room together.

Suddenly, she could only see the humor in the situation. Her frustration and humiliation disappeared, and she burst out laughing.

Her laughter wiped the smirk right off Elliot's face. His eyes widened in surprise, and he furrowed his brow in confusion.

"What's so funny?" he asked.

"Just that every time we run into each other, I'm in some strange compromising position." She laughed harder. "Except last night, of course."

"No. Then you were just trying to kill me with that oversized bag of yours. What did you have in that thing, a whole paint kit?"

Fern only laughed harder at that, and Elliot finally joined in.

"It really is funny," he admitted, and they stood together in the classroom, amused by the strangeness of their meetings. The more Fern tried to stop, the more she giggled, and Elliot's laughter was contagious, too.

The bell above the door jingled.

"Why didn't I hear that before?" Fern asked through her giggles.

"Hello?" a familiar voice called. "I think they're through here." A moment later, Thatcher walked into the room, Veronica following. They stared at Fern and Elliot.

"What's going on here?" Veronica asked.

Fern looked at Veronica and Thatcher. How could she explain everything without it sounding crazy? She glanced at

Elliot, and their eyes locked. For a moment, they stared at each other...then burst into laughter again.

Veronica and Thatcher glanced at each other in confusion.

"And to think, I thought Fern might be crazy," Thatcher said, a smile playing around his lips. "But it looks like Elliot has lost his marbles, too."

The statement only made Elliot and Fern laugh harder, and Veronica and Thatcher watched them with amusement. But neither of them could understand just how funny the situation was.

Fern took a deep breath and leaned against the table, finally getting ahold of her giggles. Elliot still chuckled. When they looked at the other two, their laughter finally faded, and they all stared at one another awkwardly.

# Chapter 8
# Elliot

Fern was beautiful when she laughed, and Elliot wanted more of it. When he was around her, he felt like everything fell away, and the world didn't look nearly as gray and dreary as it sometimes could.

When Thatcher and Veronica arrived, Elliot knew they wouldn't understand the inside joke he and Fern had shared. The laughter started to fade, awkward tension replacing it. Elliot cleared his throat and scratched his head, glancing between the three others standing with him in the back room.

Veronica's eyes sparkled as she looked between Elliot and Fern. "I'm glad you're both here," she said. "On the way back to Waterstead, I was thinking about all the work I have to get done, and how running between the studio and the college cuts into my time."

"You did?" Thatcher asked, looking confused.

"I did," Veronica said pointedly before looking at Elliot and then at Fern. "And I think the best thing for me would be to work on my admin at home for the next few days."

Fern frowned. "You're not going to be at the studio with me?"

"It looks to me like you did a fine job on your own today," Veronica said. "It will just get easier from here. I trust you to take care of everything. I'm just a short distance away if you really need me."

Thatcher still looked confused. "We're going to be doing a lot of work at the house. That won't bother you?"

"Aren't you and Elliot starting here at the studio?" Veronica asked, and she gave Thatcher such an obvious look, it wasn't hard for Elliot to figure out what was going on.

"Right," Thatcher said, his face lighting up as he caught her drift. "We're going to be working here, so if you need to focus on your work at the house, it only makes sense." He turned to Elliot. "It will give you the time to build everything here at the studio without us getting underfoot."

"And Fern, you'll be able to really get settled in the studio and sort out your apartment, too," Veronica added.

"That sounds...like it could work," Fern said, although she sounded a little unsure. She ran her hand through her auburn hair and shifted her weight from one foot to the other.

"Seems to me like they're trying to get us to work together," she mumbled to Elliot.

"I'm getting the same idea," he agreed quietly, jamming his hands into his jeans pockets.

When Thatcher and Veronica looked at him, Elliot cleared his throat. "Well, if you're going to leave me here, we should finalize all the work you'd like me to do now so I don't have to keep bugging you with questions."

"That's a great idea," Thatcher said.

"I have a few things I want to discuss with you, along with an estimate."

"We better get started."

"Fern and I will be in the front," Veronica said. "She made a sale, and I want to know all about it." She smiled warmly at Fern, who nodded.

The two women left the room to take care of business while Thatcher and Elliot stayed behind. Elliot didn't miss Fern glancing over her shoulder at him before she walked through the door. He smiled as he thought about spending so much time with Fern under one roof. He liked being around her. She was feisty and not scared to tell him what she thought. They had rubbed each other the wrong way, but just when it looked like they would be stuck there, they'd laughed together in perfect harmony.

How long had it been since he'd enjoyed someone's company and been intrigued by them?

Too long. He was here for work and nothing else, but it was a pleasant surprise to find someone who made him see the humor in life again.

"Where do you want to start?" Thatcher asked.

"Right here," Elliot said. "The cubbies will be here." He measured an area, pacing from one wall to the middle of the room. "And I'm thinking an extra space for canvases over here, with storage for paint here, away from the window where it can dry out in the sunlight."

"That sounds like a great idea," Thatcher said.

"We're going to have to get rid of the table, and I hear it's pretty heavy." He remembered seeing Fern flat on her face, a rope tied around her waist and the table legs, and grinned to himself. She was a character, that much was sure.

"I don't think Veronica is attached to the table," Thatcher said. "It came with the place and will just be in the way. If you can get it out through the door in one piece, we can sell it."

"I'm on it." Elliot had half a mind to buy the table himself, just because of the scene that was burned onto his frontal lobe.

"You should start in this room first, so Fern can start her classes," Thatcher said.

"That's fine. I can get started first thing as soon as I get the supplies. If you give me that deposit, I can get going." Elliot took out a calculator and worked out an estimate before showing it to Thatcher.

"That's fine," Thatcher said, nodding. "Have you had a chance to look at the office? I want you to do that next. In quick succession, if possible."

"Sure," Elliot said.

They walked through the gallery to the office on the other side. Fern and Veronica talked excitedly, discussing paintings. Fern was nodding in agreement, her eyes sparkling. When Elliot glanced at them, he noticed Veronica pointing toward him.

They were discussing him.

What could they be saying? He strained to hear, but when he and Thatcher had walked into the room, the women had dropped their voices to a low whisper that was impossible to make out.

*It doesn't matter what they're saying about me. It doesn't matter what Fern's thinking. She's a great person, but it doesn't matter what she thinks of me. We're both here for work, thrown together by chance and nothing else. I'm leaving all of this behind soon.*

Was it only by chance that they'd been thrown together, though? Elliot couldn't help but wonder. Every time they were together, they had a strange connection, and he was fascinated by the push and pull between them. Did she feel the same way about him? Was she as drawn to the strange chemistry between them as he was?

*It's just Veronica's and Thatcher's discussions about fate messing with your head.*

"Here we go," Thatcher said.

Elliot was still watching the women, and Thatcher chuckled. "Distracted, huh?"

"Not at all," Elliot said, shaking his head. "I was just

wondering about how the gallery was set up."

Thatcher grinned at him knowingly. "Women are dangerous creatures, in my humble opinion. One minute, you have your mind set with plans for the future, and the next, all those plans fly out of the window and you're more than happy to compromise on every single thing for them."

Elliot studied Thatcher. The tall, thin man with his tan skin and easy-going attitude looked downright content.

"It sounds like you're talking from experience," Elliot said.

"Oh, you bet. Let me tell you, having a woman in your life is an enormous pain in the neck and the best thing that could ever happen to you at the same time. One moment, you're thinking about your freedom, and the next, your privacy is invaded by an emotional, sobbing little bird. And then, just when you have your freedom back and you can leave it all behind, you realize that's not what you want at all."

Elliot narrowed his eyes at Thatcher, who still grinned at him.

"I only just met Fern," Elliot said.

"You're right, you're right," Thatcher said. "And you can't know anything about her in such a short time. It was the same with Veronica. You heard our story. When I met her, I thought she was downright crazy. But something about her drew me, and no matter what I did, I couldn't get away from her. Now, I'm not saying it's the same with Fern out there. For all we know, she could be a fugitive from the law, and that's not the kind of crazy you want in your life...but sometimes, you don't know what you want until it's right in front of you."

Elliot shook his head. "I'm not interested in anything. I'm here to do a job, and I intend to do it as best I can. It doesn't matter what kind of crazy she might be. I'm not looking for any extra complications in my life."

"Of course, of course," Thatcher said. "Then again, you can't always choose how fate treats you, now can you?" He grinned again before asking Elliot to show him what he had in mind for the office and the estimate for getting that work started.

While Elliot worked, he envisioned what the office would look like and knew he could make something great out of this room. He would deliver exceptional work—that was how business was done. Word of mouth was how he got his business, and he would impress Thatcher to the point the man wouldn't stop talking about his abilities as a handyman and carpenter.

He meant what he'd said—he wasn't interested in anything with Fern. She was a wonderful person, and Elliot looked forward to being in the same space with her. But that was only because he liked spending time with her. He wasn't interested in a relationship.

He'd been in a relationship once, but they'd been better off as friends. Elliot had accepted it for what it was. His parents had started out in love, but as time passed, they'd grown apart and their love had simply died.

Elliot wasn't ready for that. He wasn't ready to commit himself to someone only to lose the love he thought he would have. He'd seen the pain it caused, and he was wholly uninterested in a partnership that ended up with two people so distant from each other.

The easiest way to avoid that was to ensure he never fell for someone in the first place. And as long as he focused on his company, on expanding his business and finding new clients, he wouldn't be risking his heart. The new city and his life there, where he would have to focus on building his professional reputation, would be distraction enough.

But he couldn't help but admit that someone like Fern certainly made it harder for him, and there were times he felt lonely and wondered what it would be like to have someone like her by his side.

But a Thanksgiving dinner or Christmas at home always reminded him what he wasn't missing by being single, and that was what he would stick to.

Once Thatcher was happy with the plans, they joined Veronica and Fern in the gallery. Veronica gushed about the sale and how good Fern was at her job, and Fern blushed, her cheeks turning pink.

"Right," Veronica said after a moment. "We're headed home. We'll leave you two to it."

She and Thatcher said their goodbyes and left. Fern turned to Elliot. He cleared his throat and rubbed his hands together.

"I'll be in there, measuring and getting things ready. And maybe moving that table." He smirked at Fern as he said it, jabbing his thumb over his shoulder.

She rolled her eyes. "Well, it's about time I knock off, so I'm going to work on the apartment. I'll be upstairs if you need anything. Call me when you want to leave so I can lock up down here."

Elliot nodded. Fern left, walking away from him without looking back. He forced himself to do the same, walking into the back room to finish clearing up the space where she'd left off.

He tugged and yanked on the table, throwing his weight into it. He was much stronger than Fern and managed to get the table far enough away from the wall that he could push himself in behind it. He pushed the table further, more easily now.

When his foot hooked on something, he frowned and kneeled behind the table. A wooden floor cornice ran the length of the room. It had probably been installed to hide the joints of a wooden floor that must have been torn out years ago. Elliot noticed that a part of it jutted out further than the others.

He pried it loose with his fingers and pulled. It came out

easily. In the wooden wall itself, Elliot found a tin. He pulled it out and put it on the table. When he opened the lid, he found a few souvenirs, clearly the memories of a time long past.

Movie ticket stubs from some forty years ago. A pressed flower. A ribbon that still faintly smelled like perfume. And a few letters.

No names had been written on the envelopes.

Elliot opened one, carefully handling the old paper. It crackled under his fingers.

The loopy scrawl on the page had faded with time, and it was hard to read in places. He leaned back a little, lifting the letter toward the sunlight to better decipher it, and figured out what it said.

*My sweetheart,*

*I'm tormented by the thought of you. I called it off between us so I could get you out of my mind and learn to live a life without you. But you have bewitched me, body and soul, and I can't get you off my mind. I know I hurt you by telling you goodbye. I convinced myself that I would forget about you, that it was only a temporary setback to heal from this broken heart.*

*I was wrong. I wish I could tell you that. I wish I could show you just how wrong I was, and how broken I am without you. If I could go back into the past and change what had happened, I would. I would do it all again, and this time, I would make sure that you and I never ended.*

*But the past can't be changed. It's only the future we command, and I dread the idea of a future without you in it.*

*P.*

. . .

Elliot frowned and peered into the tin, looking at the other letters. Who had written these? And why had they been hidden away in the wall?

He wanted to read another one but decided against it. He was here to work.

He put a lid on the tin and tucked it into his bag. He wasn't taking it for good; he would just read the letters in his own time and bring them back here before the job was over.

He wondered if the couple ever found each other again, and who they were. Were they the same people Fern had talked about at dinner?

Pushing those thoughts aside, Elliot kept working. He heard Fern moving around in the apartment above him, her footsteps heavy as she carried things around, followed by a thump whenever she set something down on the floor.

A moment later, he heard a soft humming through the wooden floor above him—the sound of Fern keeping herself busy while she worked. He liked the sound of her voice. His mind wandered to the letter, to someone who'd lost a love because of a choice. Someone who hadn't realized what it meant to lose what he had.

Elliot knew he would never walk that road. He knew what love could be, and he knew he was happy without it. So many people chased after one thing and one thing only. But there was more to life than love, and he could live a full life without it.

He just had to have the right mindset.

He and Fern continued to work together, she in the apartment above, and he in the studio below. When it was time to leave, her humming stopped, and Elliot hoped it would start again. But it didn't, so he packed his things and walked upstairs to tell her she could lock up.

# Chapter 9
# Fern

Over the last two days, Fern had moved things around in the apartment, figuring out where to start to make it livable. The next morning, she woke up at the crack of dawn. It was still far too early to open the studio, to get ready and start her day, but she couldn't fall asleep again. The crisp ocean air pushed through the crack in her window, begging her to get up and greet the day.

She didn't lie in bed for a minute longer. She felt restless, uncertain. Her mind kept spinning, and she thought about home a lot. How was her mother doing? How were things going with Hank?

She forced herself to stop thinking about the life she'd left behind. She'd left Houston for a reason. She needed to carve out her own space here where she could belong, and that was what she would focus on.

After a quick shower, she got dressed and packed a bunch of cleaning products in the trunk of her car. She drove through the town's quiet streets; everyone else was still asleep. It was already light out, but the sun was still below the horizon, bathing the town in a surreal, shimmering light. Fog swirled in the corners of houses as she drove through the deserted streets.

Being the only one awake gave Fern a sense of privacy she hadn't felt in the town before. She found herself enjoying the drive to the Airbnb with no one spotting her and watching where she was going.

She'd been watched her whole life, having to answer to Hank and his rules. Being free of all that—although it had taken her far too long to break away—made her feel like she could finally breathe.

After she parked in front of V Studios, Fern carried her cleaning supplies up to the apartment. She trod carefully on the wooden stairs, careful not to slip on the condensation the foggy night had left behind.

She unlocked the two doors before stepping into the dusty room. Today, she was going to take care of the apartment, cleaning it up as much as she could so she could start living there.

It was a dream to have a place like this. A place that belonged to her, a space she could call her own, was another of the many things she'd sacrificed by staying with her mother and dealing with the daily drama in that house.

When she glanced at the clock, Fern saw she had almost three hours before she had to open the gallery below. Hopefully, she could take care of the apartment and clean most of it before starting her workday.

She started on the piles of trash she'd put into black bags. It took three trips to take five full trash bags down to the bins before she could tackle the other tasks.

The box of letters she'd found sat on the counter in the open-plan kitchen. She glanced at them for a moment, running her fingers along the stack of envelopes that were just as she'd left them two days ago.

She'd only worked her way through a handful of letters.

Who were they from? And who were they for? How had the lovers' story ended? Fern wished she could find out the story behind the letters and discover if the two lovers had ended up together. The letters didn't give any indication of what had happened, only that a torn heart had been left behind.

Fern took one letter from the stack and opened it. She knew she would get lost in the letter again, but she couldn't help herself.

The delicate handwriting that had drawn her in before was addictive. Fern ached to know more about the writer. When she read the words, they resonated with something inside her that she didn't understand.

*Dearest,*

*I've been thinking about sacrifices a lot. Everything in life is about choices, and everything is about sacrifice. We always sacrifice one thing for another, even if it doesn't seem that way. If I choose to start working out, to lose weight and focus on my appearance, I sacrifice the luxury of eating whatever I want, of sleeping in, of resting my aching muscles.*

*Similarly, if I choose to move away for the freedom of starting over, I sacrifice the people who stay behind and the memories I've created. I have to create a new life when I've been established before.*

*Is that what this is? Are these the sacrifices I was ready for when I made my decision? It feels like after thinking everything over so many times, I didn't consider what it would really mean to take this step. I understood the definition of the word "sacrifice," but I didn't understand the emotional turmoil I would have to accept as part of my daily life.*

*Was the sacrifice worth it to you? Are you able to deal with the pain? Because the truth is, I'm not sure if I'm that happy with the choices I've made. I can't turn back now and tell anyone that I made a mistake. You know what I'm like—I can't admit to something like that. But if I had to be honest with you—and with myself—and if I had the courage and lacked the pride to admit it, I would put into so many words that I was wrong.*

*You do know me, don't you? You know how impossible it is for me to say that.*

*I'm sorry.*

*M.*

Fern read the letter again. It hit home hard. How many sacrifices had she herself made? What were the odds that she would find this letter when she'd been thinking so much about sacrifices herself?

She couldn't accept that it was as simple as that—that every sacrifice she'd made had come from a choice. Why would she have chosen to give up her dreams if she hadn't been forced to make those decisions? She felt robbed by everything she'd had to give up, and to say that she'd chosen this path was to take away the reason for her anger.

Fern wasn't ready to accept something like that and wouldn't take that burden upon herself. No matter what the letter said, and no matter how simple the writer made it sound.

She wasn't in the same position as the writer of the letter.

What had the reply been? Fern wished once more that she had the other letters, that she could see the other side of the conversation.

Footsteps on the stairs yanked Fern from her train of thought, and she froze. Her breathing came faster, becoming erratic and shallow. Was it Hank? How had he found her? Fear clutched at her throat. If he found her here, he would take out his anger on her. She'd left Houston without telling anyone where she was going—not even her mother knew, and she'd kept it that way for a reason. She'd fled the city like a thief in the night to embark on a new life that was safer than the world she'd left behind.

But he'd found her, hadn't he? The fear clutching at her made her mind switch off, and her body took over. Blood rushed into her ears, her heartbeat rose to her throat, and she broke out in a cold sweat.

She had to protect herself somehow.

She looked around, frantically searching for a makeshift defensive weapon. Hank was big and strong, and there was nothing more dangerous than a man who didn't care about the destruction he left in his wake. He would use every bit of his strength to teach her a lesson, and this time, she'd really messed up in his eyes.

Fern spotted an umbrella and grabbed it. She shook off the cobwebs on it, the fear of Hank overriding her fear of any creepy crawlies. She held the umbrella like a bat over her shoulder and hid behind the open door. Her heart thundered against her ribs as the footsteps reached the top of the stairs, stepped into the foyer, and came closer and closer.

Fern was nearly blinded with fear when the intruder appeared in the doorway. She jumped out with a cry, the umbrella above her head, and struck. The intruder jumped back; she'd just missed him.

Fern started screaming, a battle cry that she desperately hoped would compensate for her fear. The intruder started screaming, too.

She swung and missed again, but she wouldn't relent. On the third swing, she finally hit something.

"Fern!" the man shouted. "Stop! Stop!" He grabbed the umbrella. "It's me, Elliot!"

His words pushed through her fear, and she stopped fighting. She stared at him, stunned.

"Elliot?" she asked.

"You can't change my mind now," Elliot said. "I'm convinced you're trying to kill me."

Fern stared at Elliot. It wasn't Hank who'd found her; it was Elliot, who'd come up the stairs just to talk to her. She wasn't in danger, and she'd just attacked him with an umbrella.

The immediate danger was gone, and the adrenaline pumping through her veins started to subside. At last, her heartbeat slowed, and in the void left behind by the fear, laughter bubbled up her throat.

How many times would she and Elliot be caught in these bizarre situations?

Her laughter became almost hysterical, and her body and mind reset itself, understanding that there was no danger.

Elliot began to laugh, too. "You're crazy."

Fern didn't even take offense to that statement—she *had* acted like a madwoman just then. "You should have seen the look on your face." She laughed.

Elliot shook his head, still laughing. He put his hand on his other arm and winced as he rotated his shoulder.

Fern stopped laughing, realizing she'd hurt him. If he hadn't managed to dodge two of her swings, he would have been in a lot more pain. She'd meant to protect herself, no matter what it took. A pang of guilt shot through her chest.

"I hurt you," she said.

Elliot still turned his shoulder, shaking his head. "You

need better aim if that's how you're planning to protect yourself."

She blushed. Her fear had taken over, but even in her frenzy, she hadn't been able to do that much damage. If it had been Hank...she tried not to think about what that would have meant. She pushed the thoughts of Hank out of her mind completely.

"Yeah, that wasn't my finest moment," she said.

Elliot shook his head and glanced at her clothing. "And maybe consider investing in a washing machine, too."

Fern looked down at her clothes. "What?"

She saw she was once again covered in dust and grime. She'd been working with trash and dust, and she hadn't even gotten into cleaning properly.

"I have a washing machine!" she cried out.

Elliot raised his eyebrows, and his look of disbelief made her laugh all over again. He shook his head, laughing again, too.

"What were you trying to do?" he asked through his laughter.

"I thought you were...someone else."

"You can be glad I'm not a customer. That would really have caused trouble for Veronica."

Fern giggled again, trying to imagine how that would have gone down. How could she have explained to Veronica that she was chasing her customers around with an umbrella? The mental image was hilarious.

She doubled over with laughter, her stomach cramping now. When she straightened up, Elliot was leaning down, too, and she bumped her head against his.

"Ow, woman!" he cried out.

She staggered back, lost her footing, and fell onto the wooden floor. A cloud of dust rose around her, and she coughed and spluttered.

Elliot gasped, and he quickly crouched to sit next to her. "Are you okay?"

"Are *you*?"

"What did I say about killing me?"

"I'm just so clumsy," Fern said, giggling. She leaned in a little closer and pressed her fingers against Elliot's head, probing him softly.

"Ah," he said with a wince, and she withdrew her hand.

"Sorry," she said.

The laughter subsided, and Fern suddenly became aware of how close they were to each other. Their faces were inches apart, their bodies close enough that a mere sigh could push them together.

The atmosphere shifted, and Fern's breath caught in her throat. Her laughter had faded completely, and she looked into his hazel eyes. There were golden flecks in them, and they gazed at her somberly.

Her throat closed. Elliot's closeness was warm and comforting, but at the same time, it scared her. She hadn't been this close to a man in a long, long time. The only closeness she'd had to someone all these years was Hank... when he laid a hand on her to grab her, to shake her, to show her how wrong she'd been and that she needed to be punished.

The fear she'd experienced earlier crept up on her, and no matter how much she told herself that this was Elliot and he wouldn't do anything to her, she couldn't help but fear him.

And with that fear came a whole lot of guilt and uncertainty. Had Hank ruined her for a happy life? Had he made her fear all men? She *knew* Elliot wouldn't hurt her, that he was nothing like Hank—the moment she'd met him, she sensed he was kind and sweet, albeit frustrating and pompous at times. And yet, it was as if her body had a different idea of what was real. Despite knowing these things, her body grew cold with fear, and she had to fight the urge to run and hide, to get away from him.

Her eyes stung with tears, and she swallowed hard to get rid of the lump in her throat. She tried not to cower away from Elliot. The last thing she wanted—after she'd already hurt him, twice—was to make him think that he'd done something wrong. He was a nice person, for crying out loud. Nice enough that Veronica and Thatcher wanted to set them up with each other. Her new friends wouldn't want to do that if Elliot was dangerous.

*You don't know anything about him. What if he's dangerous and they don't know any better than I do? What if they have it all wrong, too, and this is something I should run away from?*

She couldn't get herself to think straight. Two sides of her mind warred with each other—one side reminded her that she was far from Houston and the difficulties there. She had nothing to fear, and she had no reason to be as torn up as she was right now. The other half told her that she knew where things could lead, and she had to get away while she still could. She couldn't allow someone to get close enough to hurt her the way Hank had, and she couldn't allow someone to get close enough to control her life the way Hank controlled her mother.

Time slowed down, and she could see concern in Elliot's eyes. She didn't want him to feel guilty for hurting her in any way, especially not since she'd been the one to hurt him, technically. But she couldn't shake herself from the emotions that threatened to overwhelm her. She didn't know how to tell herself that the what-ifs happening in her mind weren't happening right now.

She realized with a shock that she would never get away. No matter how far she ran from Houston, no matter how much pain she tried to leave behind, it would follow her everywhere. The fear, the memories, the reactions. They would all catch up with her, even if she ran to the ends of the earth.

She'd been running all this time, but she hadn't escaped at all.

# Chapter 10
# Elliot

He wasn't sure what was going on, but this wasn't how it was meant to be. With Fern so close to him, the first thing Elliot thought was that he wanted to kiss her. He'd told himself he wasn't going to get involved with anyone—he didn't want love, he didn't want a partner, he didn't want companionship.

But now that she was so close to him, all he could think was that he wanted her closer. He wanted to know what it would feel like if he pressed his lips against hers.

Except, that magical moment seemed to be magical only to him. For a moment, she'd looked as entranced as he was, but then, her eyes changed. They filled with what he could only describe as fear, and he could see the pulse in her throat quicken. Her breathing became shallow, and even though she was looking into his eyes, he was sure she saw something else there.

Elliot didn't want to force whatever demons she was fighting on her even more. So, instead of leaning forward and brushing his lips against hers, he backed away and pushed himself up to stand. It was probably better this way, anyway. If he kissed her, he might become more involved than he wanted to be, and he didn't want to complicate things.

He held out a hand to her. Fern glanced at it, looking uncertain.

He dropped his hand to his side. He wasn't going to put any pressure on her to do anything that made her even more uncomfortable. He recognized all the signs. In Fern, he saw a woman who'd been hurt. He saw an echo of his sister.

She struggled to her feet, nearly falling again. Elliot was about to step forward and help, but he stopped himself.

Finally, she got to her feet and glanced at him. Now that they were both standing, she swallowed hard and turned away. She looked embarrassed about something.

"Here," he said, handing her the umbrella.

"Thanks," she said, holding it in front of her like a protective barrier.

*What did this woman go through that she's so scared of something as simple as laughing with a friend? The one thing I can't do is ask her outright, but I wish I knew how to make her feel better.*

Elliot hated it when a woman was in distress and he couldn't do anything to be the hero. He pushed his hands into his pockets and stepped away to put more distance between them.

What was going on with her? Her behavior made him feel terrible. He knew she wasn't acting this way because of anything he'd done. A woman behaving like this had been through a lot more than just one or two strange interactions. But he hated that he had somehow reminded her of whoever or whatever it was that scared her so much. He didn't want to bring pain to anyone.

With that regret came a wave of anger. Who could have hurt her enough to make her fear Elliot when he'd done nothing to her? He'd seen battered women before. His sister's good-for-nothing ex-husband had hurt her for years before Elliot had finally stepped in. It made him see red to know a man might have used his strength against someone as delicate and beautiful as Fern.

Elliot had told himself that he would never do anything to make a woman feel that way, and now it had just happened.

"I should get going," he said.

"I should open up the studio anyway," she said in a brittle voice.

"I'll come back later to figure out the work on the apartment. You let me know when will be good for you."

Fern nodded and pursed her lips together.

"Look, I'm sorry I scared you," he said. "I didn't mean to do that."

"Don't be sorry," she said.

But Elliot was sorry, because it wasn't right that she was going through this.

"You have a good day," he said, turning away from her and walking toward the door. When he was in the foyer, he hesitated. Should he leave her alone right now? Perhaps it was better that he left her now so she could pull herself together before facing customers.

When he stepped out onto the stairs, he thought he heard a sob coming from the apartment. He started to go back and make sure Fern was okay, but he stopped himself. Instead, he forced himself to climb down the stairs and put more and more distance between them. It crushed him to know that he'd upset her this much. How could he have let something like this happen? It hadn't been his fault, but he still felt awful.

He got into his car, not knowing where to go. He could pick up supplies for Thatcher and start on the office later, he decided. It would be okay for him to work there, even when Fern was in the gallery. He just needed to give her some space.

He drove out of Waterstead, following the road that led to

Rockport. He would go to his workshop and collect a few tools there. After, he would stop at his place and grab more clothes. He was going to be in Waterstead a bit longer than he'd initially planned.

But he would do what needed to be done. He wanted to do a good job, and he wanted to be closer to Fern for a while. Knowing she wasn't okay awoke his protective side. He wanted to be sure she would get through whatever it was she was struggling with.

He felt guilty again for what had happened. He reviewed everything he'd said and done, trying to figure out where he might have gone wrong and triggered an upsetting memory. But she'd been giggling the one moment and then terrified the next. She must have already been in a bad space, as she was ready to attack him when he'd arrived.

In the future, he would announce himself better so he wouldn't surprise her. He remembered how jumpy his sister had been, and he wasn't going to be the reason Fern panicked if he could help it.

Thinking those things only made him feel marginally better. He still wanted to be there for her, and he still felt terrible for how he'd made her feel.

He would do better. He didn't know if he could help her, but he knew he couldn't make it any worse.

That was something.

# Chapter 11
# Fern

The classroom was going to be Fern's sanctuary; she already knew it. This was where she would teach students how to paint and share everything she'd learned. It was a gift to bring emotion to life with color and light, and she wanted to impart that gift to others.

Helping others find a way to escape, a way to communicate without words, excited Fern. If she could give that to others, she would feel fulfilled.

The cubbies would soon be installed, and she'd overheard something about Elliot wanting to add a projector and a screen. It was a wonderful idea—she could teach that much easier if she could work with slides. She was impressed with how Elliot considered his clients and offered extra input.

He was a good man. Even when her body didn't always agree.

After Elliot had gone, she'd taken a chance and left the studio closed a short while longer. Instead, she'd driven to the hardware store, where she'd bought black paint. Now, after the close of the business day, she painted the walls black as music blared into her ears. She wasn't going back to the apartment just yet. She wanted to keep cleaning, but after this morning, she needed a distraction.

Fern became lost in her own world. She sang along to the song blasting on the speakers, painting the walls in broad strokes. The act of painting felt so soothing and therapeutic.

"You're painting the walls black?" Veronica's voice sounded right behind her.

Fern jumped and spun around. When she saw it was Veronica, she turned down the music.

"I didn't hear you come in," she said.

"With the music on, I don't blame you," Veronica said with a smile.

Fern had locked the doors, and with the business day over, she hadn't needed to worry about customers. Veronica had a key, which was the only reason she'd been able to sneak up on Fern.

"Sorry," Fern said.

"Not at all." Veronica shook her head and glanced around the room. "Interesting choice of color."

"Oh, yeah. I know it's a little unorthodox, but look." She turned to the paintings that leaned against the far wall, which she hadn't put up yet. She held one up against the wall she'd been working on, careful not to touch the wet paint. "What do you think?"

Veronica studied the picture. "I see what you're doing. It really makes the colors pop."

"That's what I want," Fern admitted. "I want the students to see that with a little extra work, they can drive a whole new feeling home that wasn't there before. Art isn't only in the art itself but in its presentation."

"That's very good," Veronica said, nodding.

"A monochromatic color scheme does a lot for the color in the artwork," Fern continued. "And it looks so sophisticated. It allows us to work on a whole new level of customers, too. If you design your website the same way, then it can really come together, and you could draw people from much farther and wider than you are now."

Veronica blushed. "I don't have a website."

"What?!" Fern cried out. "How do you reach your clients and customers?"

Veronica shrugged. "Word of mouth, my phone number, business cards at places like the college workshop..."

"We could do a lot more marketing and reach a whole new group of people."

"I think we should look into that," Veronica said, nodding. "I keep finding more and more reasons why it was a great idea to hire you!"

Fern smiled, pleased with herself. She hadn't been trying to show off, but it looked like she could bring a lot more to the table than she'd initially thought. It made her feel like she could make a difference and the move had been worth it.

"I've done this before," Fern said, waving at the black walls. "I decorated my home in Houston the same way, and it made a big difference."

She didn't add how angry Hank had been about the black walls and how her mom had asked her what the point was, which had led to an argument that sparked one of her mom's episodes.

Everything back home left a bad taste in her mouth.

"How are we going to find students?" Veronica asked.

Fern was glad for the change of topic. "Well, I've been looking around on student forums and already reached out to a few students. The sooner we can get the classroom done, the better. I've signed five students up so far."

Veronica blinked at Fern. "What?"

"Is that okay?" Fern asked, suddenly nervous that she'd done something wrong. "I thought we were going to jump right in, so I took the liberty—"

"No, no, it's great! I just can't believe how proactive and *dynamic* you are. I thought this thing would take months to get it up and running, and you already have *five* students."

Fern nodded slowly. "People are eager to learn if they just have somewhere they can go."

"What else have you done?" Veronica asked.

"Well…I've been hired for two commissions today. They're portraits, so not very inventive, but it's bread and butter kind of stuff, you know? So, I'll be working on those soon. I've also talked to a few customers who came in about the paintings, so I think we'll get at least one sale out of that."

Veronica shook her head, impressed. "It looks like you've really hit the ground running."

"I love it here," Fern admitted. "I didn't realize how fulfilling it would be. I love art so much, I don't feel like I'm working at all. It's just a pleasure being here."

"It's a pleasure having you here."

Fern felt warm at those words.

"Did Elliot stop by today?" Veronica asked, and Fern's stomach dropped. "Thatcher told me what he wants to do to the place, and I really like his ideas. What do you think about them?"

"The cubbies and stuff?" Fern asked, glancing at the wall where they would be installed.

Veronica nodded. "I'm especially excited about the way he wants to set up the office. His ideas could really help us stay organized and make this thing work."

Her excitement set Fern more at ease. She didn't know what to say about her last run-in with Elliot. Had he said anything to Veronica about what had happened in the apartment that morning? But Veronica chatted on, and it didn't seem like he'd said anything at all. Fern was relieved— she was mortified by how she'd acted, and she still felt emotionally fragile after her memories had trampled her.

"He was here, but not for long," Fern finally answered. "It does seem like he knows what he's doing, and I think his work could make the place great. He can complete it and make it look as sophisticated as I would like the rest of the studio to be."

Veronica nodded excitedly. "I think so, too! I really like the whole thing. When Thatcher said he would get someone in, I was worried about what it would mean. Thatcher was the one who wanted to do it all, you know? But I think this was the best course of action, and it's going to work out just fine."

Fern nodded in agreement. Her personal situation with Elliot was beside the point.

"I'm so glad you and Elliot get along," Veronica added, and Fern froze. "It would be awful if you didn't, and that first day, I was worried about that. The last thing I want is to make your workplace an unhappy place."

"We get along just fine," Fern said, forcing a smile.

Veronica looked pleased and didn't seem to pick up on Fern's effort to keep things light. Fern didn't want her friend to pry. She couldn't explain what she was going through, and it was easier not to talk about it so that she could move forward. The moment she went into detail about it, she felt like she would sound ridiculous or say something that would make the whole thing seem more dramatic than it needed to be.

She wasn't a damsel in distress, and she didn't want anyone to think she was.

Veronica looked around, nodding to herself. She was pleased with what Fern had done so far, and it made Fern feel like she could offer something more than she'd thought when first arriving here. Fern was happy that, despite all her problems, she could still bring something to the table.

"This could really be great," she said to Veronica. "I didn't think I would feel as at home here as I do. Was it like that for you, too?"

"Absolutely," Veronica said. "When I first came here, it was on a whim. After all, thinking about moving onto Thatcher's property was terrifying. I'd lost a whole lot before. But now…"

She smiled, and Fern felt a stab of envy at the contentment on Veronica's face. It wasn't that she didn't want her friend to be happy—on the contrary, it was exactly what she wanted. But finding that same kind of happiness felt nearly impossible for her.

*The happiness you're after isn't love. You want your freedom, and that's what you're getting. Your behavior around Elliot this morning is proof enough that a relationship isn't something you'd be good at right now.*

"I can't believe how things are between me and Thatcher," Veronica said with a contented sigh. "When I left my home, running away from everything that haunted me, I couldn't have guessed in a million years that I would find this kind of happiness."

"You ran away?" Fern asked in surprise.

Veronica nodded. "Oh, yes. You see, I lost my husband and son in a terrible car accident, and for a long time, I was a mess. I didn't leave the house, I lost my friends. Things just got worse and worse, and I lived in perpetual darkness."

"I can't believe you went through something so terrible!" Fern cried. "I'm so sorry."

Veronica shook her head with a sad smile. "There is nothing to be sorry about. It's in the past—these things do happen sometimes. It was when things became unbearable that I decided to throw a few belongings into a car and hit the road. I didn't even know where I was going. When I had car trouble, I was stranded on the side of a deserted highway and thought this was it, that things couldn't get any worse.

But then, like an angel, Thatcher arrived and helped me out."

Fern shook her head, awed to hear how things had worked out for Veronica and Thatcher. She had known their story was special; it had to be, with their connection to each other. But this...this was so different than what she could have imagined.

If something so good could come of something so horrible in Veronica's life...a spark of hope ignited within Fern. Could she find happiness amid her own darkness?

"I'm so happy things are better for you now," Fern said.

"Oh, sometimes it's still difficult. Thatcher and I have our moments where we don't understand each other. It's a new relationship, after all. And I still struggle with the past at times. I miss my late husband and son so much, sometimes I feel like I can't breathe. But in time, things get better. Time heals all wounds, doesn't it?"

Fern nodded. "They do say that." She just wasn't sure her own wounds could heal with time, no matter how much time she got.

Veronica put her hand on Fern's shoulder as if she knew what she was thinking. "You're going to get through whatever is bugging you, I can promise you that. It doesn't always stay so difficult."

"How do you know it will work out like that for me, too?"

"Because it will be a happy ending, Fern. And if it's not happy...it's not the end."

Veronica flashed her a dazzling smile, and Fern wanted with all her heart to believe her new friend. She was still afraid, but she had to push through. There was no other way to do it. If she had to choose between moving forward and looking back, she would keep moving forward.

When Fern finished at the studio, she decided to drop by Linda's place and take the woman up on her offer to get involved with one of her projects. When Fern walked into the haberdashery, Linda stood behind the counter, flipping through a magazine. She looked up when Fern walked in.

"Oh! Fern, it's so good to see you. I was hoping you would drop by."

"Really?" Fern asked, surprised. It felt good that the woman had wanted to see her. It always felt good to feel like she belonged.

"Absolutely. I just got a whole load of secondhand clothing in, and it needs to be sorted and distributed among the needy. Do you think this is something you might be interested in?"

"I would," Fern said, nodding eagerly. The best way to get involved in the community was to do something like this, and she was a whizz at organizing and sorting out. After all, that was what she was doing with the studio apartment, too.

It felt good to do something that made a difference, and working with her hands allowed her to stop thinking about the past. It was therapy for her.

"Great," Linda said. "Follow me, I'll show you where the boxes are, and we can get started."

Fern followed Linda out of the shop and into the charity store next door. It looked a lot less organized than the haberdashery, with boxes stacked all over the place and shelves that were only partially stocked.

"It's not much right now, but we are working on that," Linda said. "I don't pay people to help me, so I rely on those who are willing to help without getting anything in return." She glanced over her shoulder. "I hope that's what you had in mind."

"That's exactly what I had in mind," Fern said, nodding.

Linda smiled at Fern before pointing out the boxes. "These are all filled with clothes that need to be sorted into gender and size, and then we can drop them off at homes or send them to other charity stores where they might be needed."

"I'll get right on it," Fern said.

"Right now?" Linda asked, taken aback. "It's quite late."

"I'll do a bit tonight and then come back tomorrow after work to keep going, if that's okay with you."

"Of course," Linda said, pulling a box closer. "We'll work together."

"Oh, you don't have to stay," Fern said. "Just because I'm willing to work late doesn't mean you have to."

"Nonsense. I don't have anyone waiting for me at home. Not since Patrick passed away. It's good to stay busy—it keeps my mind off things."

Linda had no idea how close that was to how Fern felt, too. After the day she'd had, Fern didn't want to go back to the Airbnb and be alone with her thoughts. Doing something good with her time was a much better way to escape memories that would only bring her down.

She was excited to get to know Linda a little better, too. And if she kept going like this, focusing on the positive and doing something good every day, her whole life would look different in no time at all.

# Chapter 12
# Elliot

"Is this a good time?" Michelle Cameron asked when Elliot answered his phone.

"Yes, I can talk." Before standing, he put down his power tools where he was sanding the floor in the beach house. "How are you?"

"Great," Michelle said, and he could hear the smile in her voice. "I found a couple of houses I think you'll be happy with, and they're in different locations so you'll have the pick of the litter."

Michelle was a go-getter, working hard and fast. Elliot had known from the moment he'd appointed her as his real estate agent that she would do what she could to find him what he needed.

"That sounds good," Elliot said. "Will you send them to my email?"

Michelle confirmed that she would. "How are things going on your side? Are you wrapping up your loose ends before the big move?"

"They're going well enough," Elliot said. "I'm excited about the new chapter."

That wasn't entirely true. He'd been excited about the move, about starting over, but that was before he met Fern, Veronica, and Thatcher. Now, he was feeling more and more torn about the choices he'd made. It wasn't that he wanted to stay behind; he knew full well what it meant to start over, and he'd been planning this move for a long time. But Fern was so vulnerable and hurt. A protective part of him wanted to stay and make sure she was okay.

He had no idea where that impulse came from, or why he felt so strongly about her.

*This is exactly why I didn't want to get involved—I knew it would affect my plans to move away from here. She's just another battered woman. She doesn't have to be my problem.*

He didn't see her as a problem, though, and that *was* the problem. He wanted to look after her, keep her safe. It was hard to balance what he thought he needed and what he knew he wanted.

"As soon as you look at the options I've sent you, we can head out and look at the places so you can decide," Michelle said brightly.

"That sounds good," Elliot said, and they ended the call. But as he tucked his phone into his pocket, he realized he didn't feel nearly as elated as he thought he would about reviewing his housing options.

He kneeled on the wooden floor again and picked up his power tools. He turned the sander on, and the noise drowned out his thoughts.

Working with his hands had always been therapeutic. He had started woodworking as a hobby to take his mind off his problems, especially after finding out his sister was being abused. That hobby had expanded into something much bigger—he had a successful company now. But that didn't change the fact that he liked working with his hands, that getting down to the nitty-gritty and completing a project fulfilled him.

Lately, he had handed a lot of the work to his team. He'd nearly forgotten why he'd started and how much he loved it.

As he sanded the wooden floorboards, his mind drifted back to his life at home, before he'd moved into his own place. He'd grown up in Rockport. He barely remembered his life in Chicago because he had been so young. All he remembered was that his parents had been happy then, and they weren't happy in Rockport. They hadn't been happy for a long time.

Elliot had always loved the ocean and the coast. It was calming, soothing. There was something about the ocean that was so untamed. It was a beast that could be as nasty and unforgiving as it was beautiful. It was temperamental, and Elliot knew to respect it.

He'd always thought it was ironic that he loved something as volatile as the ocean when that volatility was exactly what he wanted to escape. But the type of volatility he wanted to escape from was unpredictable, whereas the ocean, as moody as she was, always remained the same in what she would do.

He switched off the sanding machine and studied his handiwork. The porch was beautiful, with its incredible view of the private beach. Fixing it up until it was like new again was a pleasure.

Elliot wanted to restore the house to its former glory. It had started out as a job, but as he'd gotten to know Veronica and Thatcher better and learned their story of how they met, he wanted to do excellent work for their sakes. They deserved all that was good and beautiful in the world.

He walked into the house to wash his hands. He was covered in sawdust, so he dusted himself off before walking into the building.

A car pulled into the driveway, and Elliot looked through the kitchen window while rinsing his hands with water.

Veronica and Fern sat in the car talking and laughing as Veronica parked.

Elliot's stomach twisted. He was unsure about seeing Fern. He'd been avoiding her for the last couple of days, finding an excuse to work at the beach house again so he wouldn't run into her at the studio. He'd told himself he could work at the studio as long as he stayed out of her way, but he hadn't done that. Not with the fear he'd seen in her eyes.

What would he say to her now? He still hated that he'd been the one to remind her of her difficult past. Was it coincidence, or was there something about him that brought back her pain? He hoped it was the former but was terrified it was the latter.

And that was why he'd opted to stay away from her completely.

Buster barked from somewhere outside, the sound loud and rumbling.

"Oh no!" Veronica cried out, still outside.

He saw the dog shoot toward the two women as they climbed out of the car. He was heading straight for Fern.

"Buster, no! Brace yourself, Fern!" Veronica shouted.

Elliot watched as the large, hairy dog jumped onto Fern. She cried out as she lost her footing and fell back against the car before Buster could tackle her to the ground.

"Hey, Bus, stop it!" Veronica cried out, grabbing Buster's collar to pull him off Fern.

The big dog wouldn't budge. He licked Fern's face with a large pink tongue, happily ignoring Veronica's attempts to get him off.

Elliot's protective instincts kicked in, overtaking his reluctance to see Fern again. He ran out of the house, running down the stairs two at a time.

"Buster!" Elliot shouted, running to the Saint Bernard. He

grabbed Buster's collar with both hands and wrestled him off Fern, succeeding since he was much stronger than Veronica.

Buster didn't look put out at all. He sat down, proud of himself, panting with his pink tongue lolling out of his mouth.

"Are you okay?" Elliot asked Fern, holding out a hand to help her up. She took it, and he was relieved she didn't push him away.

"I've been better." She groaned as he pulled her to her feet. She looked down at herself and saw she was covered in mud and dog hair. "Although I'm starting to think I'm doomed for you to always see me like this—a mess."

Veronica giggled, and Elliot chuckled despite himself. He couldn't help but laugh at the situation. Fern was right—she always seemed to be covered in grime when they ran into each other.

Fern looked up at him, surprised that he was laughing. Laughter danced in her eyes, too.

"I can't even attribute this to my clumsiness," she said. "I think this was all Buster."

"Try living with him," Veronica said. "My life is now covered in dog hair."

They laughed again, and it broke the tension between Elliot and Fern. He was relieved to see her laughing. She was beautiful, even when covered in grime. The redness on her cheeks from her laughter only made her more incredible to look at. Elliot could stare at her forever.

A truck pulled up behind Veronica, and Thatcher got out.

"What's going on here?" he asked, sauntering toward the group.

"Buster is up to his usual antics," Veronica said, her voice filled with laughter. "He trampled Fern—look at her!"

They all looked at Fern.

"Don't look at me!" Fern cried out, and they all laughed again.

"Buster, you silly pup," Thatcher said affectionately, ruffling the fur on Buster's neck. "I'm sorry, Fern. I can't even tell you that we'll train this out of him. He's on the older side, and old habits die hard."

"Oh, it's okay," Fern said. "I know you can't teach an old dog new tricks."

Elliot and Thatcher laughed, and Veronica shook her head.

"Come on, Fern," Veronica said. "Let's get you cleaned up. Come to my cottage and we'll get you ready for dinner."

Elliot watched the two women walk off.

Thatcher chuckled next to him. "It's always an adventure with that dog, let me tell you."

"Did Veronica mention dinner?" Elliot asked.

"Oh, yeah, she invited Fern to come over for dinner. Of course, you're invited, too."

Elliot wasn't sure if he should stay. He was hungry and didn't feel like ordering in at the hotel or going to a restaurant alone. He didn't want to make Fern uncomfortable, either. But she hadn't looked nearly as emotional and disoriented as when he'd seen her last, and she'd even laughed about her death-by-gentle-giant experience with Buster. Still, Elliot was worried about her.

Not that he could say anything about it to Thatcher. He didn't want to embarrass Fern even more by telling the other man how she'd reacted. Elliot knew from experience that the pain that came with abuse was tough to deal with in private, let alone when others also knew about it. Tina had always hated getting sympathetic looks and pity, and people usually reacted with pity when finding out about the abuse.

No, he would brave dinner and stick it out with Fern. Whenever she looked uncomfortable, he would do what he could to make things easier for her. It was the only way to handle things without being rude and declining a dinner invitation without a good reason.

"Let me show you what I've been doing," Elliot said to Thatcher, and the two men climbed the stairs into the house, Buster short on their heels. The dog's heavy panting could be heard as they walked through the house to the porch. Buster collapsed into his basket on the porch with a heavy sigh.

"Oh, this looks grand," Thatcher said with a pleased grin. "The varnish peeling up made it look so neglected. It's like a brand-new floor."

"It's amazing what a bit of sanding and a fresh lick of varnish can do," Elliot agreed. "I'll varnish tomorrow."

"That sounds great," Thatcher said. "Something to drink?"

"Something cool would be great," Elliot confirmed.

Thatcher walked to the kitchen and returned with two cold beers. He cracked one open and handed it to Elliot before opening his own.

"We'll switch over to iced tea when the women arrive," Thatcher said. "But a cold beer after a long day is just what the soul needs."

Elliot took a long draw from the bottle. The cold beer was like an elixir down his throat.

Thatcher looked at the bottle in his hand. "I see you and Fern are getting along alright."

Elliot glanced at him, unsure how to respond to that. "She's very sweet," he finally said.

"Praise indeed," Thatcher said with a grin.

Elliot shook his head. "I know you and Veronica think we're a good match—and we could be, I won't deny that. But I'm not looking for anything serious. I'm not ready to get involved with anyone."

He didn't know if he could give Fern what she needed. He

didn't know the extent of what she'd been through, and so far, he'd seemed to scare her more than anything else. But he did like her.

"Love is a funny thing," Thatcher remarked, holding his beer bottle against his chest. "When I met Veronica, I wasn't looking for anything, either. I had the worst example of love from my parents—my father was abusive, and my mother never drew a line to leave him. In her final hours, in fact, she called out to him. It hurt me a lot to see. But now that I have Veronica in my life, I can't believe how different our relationship is from what my parents had, and I would never have known it if I hadn't given it a chance."

Elliot shook his head. "I'm not looking for anything. I'm leaving soon, and I'm not ready to get involved. Fern is a wonderful person, but I don't know if I can take on another adventure right now."

Thatcher sipped his beer, thinking. "I only have one piece of advice for you."

"What's that?"

"Follow your heart," Thatcher said simply. "It will lead you to the right place."

Elliot nodded, sipping his own beer. It wasn't as simple as Thatcher made it sound. Elliot could follow his heart if he knew what his heart wanted, but now that he'd come to this crossroads where he had to decide which way to turn, he didn't know how to figure out the answer.

And Fern had a lot going on in her life, too. If circumstances were different, maybe they could have tried for something between them, but she was clearly running away from a past that didn't want to leave her alone. The last thing she needed was Elliot complicating her life even more.

The women returned from the cottage, stepping onto the freshly sanded porch. Veronica beamed at Thatcher and walked over to him, planting a kiss on his lips.

"I'll get dinner ready," she announced before disappearing back into the house.

Fern stepped onto the porch, and she looked like a vision. She'd borrowed one of Veronica's tops, and with her jeans, she looked radiant. She'd pulled her hair back into a ponytail, which only made her large green eyes stand out more.

"Better?" she asked Elliot, turning for him to see her outfit. "Mud-free."

"Very nice," Elliot said with a chuckle.

Fern's cheeks reddened, and Elliot smiled at her.

Thatcher pointed out the excellent job Elliot had done on the porch, which led to Fern fussing over how good he was at his work, making him feel just as flattered as she'd looked when he'd complimented her.

"I think you got the perfect guy for the job," she said to Thatcher. "He's going to make this place incredible. And with this view..." She trailed off and stared out over the water.

Elliot studied her face. She was trying to put on a nonchalant smile, but in her eyes, he could see a storm brewing. She was still not completely okay after that moment in her apartment. He wished he could do something to make her feel better.

Fern cleared her throat and turned, pushing away whatever was bothering her. She looked brightly at Elliot.

"I think I'll see if Veronica needs help," she said, disappearing into the house.

Thatcher looked at Elliot without saying anything, but Elliot knew what was on the man's mind.

"Dinner's ready!" Veronica called out after several minutes.

The men walked to the dining room, which needed as much work as everything else. But the table was beautifully decorated, with a vase of wildflowers in the center and a pitcher of iced tea.

Fern poured everyone the iced tea while Veronica arranged a salad bowl and a platter of ciabatta around the vase. They dished up steak from the kitchen and sat down around the table.

"This looks incredible," Fern said to Veronica as she served herself some salad and a slice of bread.

Elliot and Thatcher waited for the women to get food before loading their plates.

"I swung by Linda's shop a few days ago," Fern said, taking a sip of iced tea. "I'm helping her with distribution. She got a whole load of clothing she wants to send out. It feels so good to help with something that will make a difference."

"I'm so glad you got involved," Veronica said. "Linda mentioned you stopped by."

"Is there a place in town where I can donate a few things?" Elliot asked, lowering his fork to his plate.

"Linda has a charity shop in town, and she's involved with all kinds of projects," Fern said.

"That's great. I'll load up some things when I go back to Rockport for more supplies."

With the move coming, Elliot had been cleaning out the clutter he'd accumulated over the years. He hated throwing things away when someone else could benefit from them.

"Why don't you get involved with the shop, too?" Veronica suggested. "Fern can show you the ropes."

"Oh, I—" Elliot began.

"It's a good idea," Thatcher said. "It's always a nice feeling to know where your things are going and the good they're doing."

Thatcher and Veronica exchanged glances, and Elliot knew they were trying to set up him and Fern again. As much as he appreciated the well-meaning gesture, Elliot wished they would let it go. He'd made it clear to Thatcher that he wasn't interested in anything.

"I could show you where it is," Fern said to Elliot.

He looked at her, and there was something hopeful in her eyes. Something that pulled him up short. Did she want to spend time with him? After what had happened between them, it was hard to imagine, but he didn't want to shut her down. It wasn't easy for her to reach out, he was sure.

"Okay," he conceded.

Veronica looked pleased, and Thatcher drank his iced tea.

Elliot wasn't sure he was ready to get this involved with a charity—it wasn't exactly his forte. But Fern would be there, and that would make all the difference.

And if it did some good...why not?

# Chapter 13
# Fern

Linda was glad to see Fern enter her shop after her shift at V Studios.

"I've come to look forward to our little visits, Fern," Linda said warmly. "I can't tell you how happy I am we're doing this together. It feels like more than just work."

Fern nodded. "I feel the same! I love making a difference, but this has started to feel like a meeting between friends."

"Exactly right," Linda said. "Come, look at this." She beckoned Fern over to a display case with jewelry, pointing to an ivory brooch that sat between other necklaces and bracelets in desperate need of cleaning.

"Oh, it's beautiful," Fern breathed.

Linda nodded. "This was mine once, you know."

"What?" Fern asked, confused. "What do you mean?"

A smile played around Linda's lips, and her eyes changed like she was looking at memories from a time long gone.

"A long time ago, when I was very young and very in love, my beau gave me this brooch as a token of his affection. I wore it all the time, no matter what I had on that day. From dressing up to go to the pictures to staying at home in loungewear, I wore this brooch on my chest."

"What happened?' Fern asked, already immersed in the story. "How did you lose it?"

"I didn't lose it," Linda said simply. "I gave it away. He broke it off with me, and I was heartbroken and furious. After a lot of anger and frustration, I got rid of the brooch because the memories were too painful." She laughed. "Do you see that little chip?" She pointed out an imperfection in the ivory. "I threw it at his head when he called it off! It's a miracle it didn't break altogether." She laughed again.

"It's a wonder you can laugh about it," Fern said.

"Oh, that pain is so far in the past. I've lived a full life, and what happened to me—what happened between us back then —shaped me as a person. I don't regret anything. I loved with reckless abandon, and although it hurt like nothing I'd felt before when I lost my love, I would go back and do it all again. It's a gift to love so purely."

Fern studied the brooch again. The love story was so sweet and yet so sad. She was about to ask how Linda had met Patrick, the man she'd spent the rest of her life with, when the door opened and a stack of boxes came through. Behind the boxes, Elliot grunted and groaned.

"Oh!" Fern cried out. "I didn't realize you were coming today."

"I wasn't planning to," Elliot said, panting. "But I had to shoot to Rockport unexpectedly. So I thought while I'm there, I might as well pack up this stuff and bring it here." He blew out a heavy breath. "That was my workout for the week. I have a lot of junk in here. I worry it might not be useful."

"Everything is useful," Linda said.

Fern introduced Linda to Elliot. Linda mentioned she'd heard of him from Veronica—she and Veronica were close.

"We can go through this stuff together," Fern said to Elliot. "Linda will let us know where to go with it."

"Oh, I can't join you tonight," Linda said. "I have an appointment I can't miss, I'm so sorry! But here." She retrieved a list from underneath the counter and handed it to Fern. "These are the things we need the most, along with where they should go. The other categories are for the odds and ends. If you sort everything accordingly, I can pick up where you left off tomorrow morning."

Fern took the list and studied it. The instructions seemed simple enough.

"Have fun, you two," Linda said. "And thank you for the help!"

Linda left the store, and Elliot and Fern were alone. The silence between them stretched thin, growing awkward.

"Well, let's get started," Fern said brightly. After she and Elliot had dinner with Veronica and Thatcher a few nights ago, it had broken the worst of the tension between them. It had been a pleasant night, but things were still a little stiff. Elliot had seen a very vulnerable, raw side of Fern, and she wasn't sure what he thought about her. Did he think she was a nutjob? She knew she'd certainly seemed like one when he'd found her in her apartment, frantic with fear and attacking him with an umbrella.

He didn't treat her like something was wrong with her, though. She appreciated it. Despite previously jumping to conclusions about her, he was a nice guy and didn't pose a threat to her.

Not when she was in the present and didn't mistake him for Hank. She shook off the mortification that came with the thought.

"Let's see what you've got," Fern said, opening the first box.

Together, they went through the boxes. Elliot had brought

old clothes, which she added to the boxes she'd been working on with Linda. He had books, too, which she stacked on the counter since books weren't on the list. He also had a whole bunch of old tools and trinkets that they divided into categories according to the list.

When Fern opened the last box, she found a tin. "What's this?"

"Oh, that's not something I want to donate. I brought that for you," Elliot said.

"For me?" She blinked at him.

He nodded. "Open it."

When Fern opened it, it was a box filled with old memories, from ticket stubs to pressed flowers and a small parcel of letters. Frowning, she carefully lifted the letters out of the tin.

"I found it in the floorboards at the studio a while ago. You mentioned the letters you found, so I thought I would bring this to you, too.

Fern gasped. "These are more of the same letters?"

"I think they might be from the other writer," Elliot said. "Let me show you." He unfolded the letter he'd read and showed it to her.

"'P,'" Fern breathed. "The others were all signed 'M.'"

"I think it might be the other writer, although I don't know why their letters would be hidden in separate places in that old building."

"I can't believe this," Fern said, and she sat down, the tin on her lap. Elliot sat down next to her, and Fern opened a letter from the bundle.


*Sweetheart,*

. . .

*It's been months without you, and I'm starting to wither away. My pining has become a physical thing, and the people around me ask me if I'm ill. I made a mistake, my love. I should have known what we had is impossible to find. I should have understood sooner how important it was that we hold onto it.*

*Now I think it's too late. You've moved on with your life by now, I'm sure—dedicated yourself to a man who knows what he has before he decides to lose it.*

*I regret, my love. I regret losing you. I regret thinking I can command fate. I regret not being able to make this right.*

*Can you forgive me? Because I don't think I can ever forgive myself.*

*Yours, no matter how far you wander away from me.*
*P.*

Fern lowered the letter and shook her head. "I wish I knew who these people were and what happened. I can feel their pain. They both write with so much emotion."

"You think it's the same people?" Elliot asked.

"Absolutely," Fern said. "If you see the other letters, they're all the same. They're two people who lost each other and regretted it so much." She sighed heavily, the weight of the lovers' pain gripping her heart.

"I wonder if it's possible to find out who they are and what happened to them," Elliot mused. "I guess we'll never know now."

"Maybe if we can track down the history of the building, we can get an idea," Fern suggested. "I'll see what I can find out. Maybe Thatcher can help."

Elliot nodded, and Fern decided it was a good idea. It would make her feel so much better to know this story had an ending. She hoped it had been a happy one—two lovers so torn up about each other deserved to be made whole. But at least any ending would put her out of the misery of wondering all the time.

"I thought about something I'd like you to paint for me," Elliot said, changing the topic.

"Oh?" Fern asked.

Elliot nodded and stood, walking to the boxes they'd already taken care of. "I want you to paint the ocean for me. With all its emotion and fury and hope and beauty. I might not see it all the time anymore when I move, but if I have a painting of it, I can take it with me and look at it when I get homesick."

"Do you think you'll get homesick?" Fern asked.

Elliot shrugged. "I don't know. Maybe. Here is the only life I've really known, and being away from the coast...I think it could be daunting on those days when the walls are closing in."

"Do you get those days often?" Fern asked carefully.

"It's why I'm moving," Elliot said softly, and an emotion flickered across his features too quickly for Fern to read.

"I know what that can be like," Fern confided. "I'm sorry you feel so stuck that moving away from what you love is the only option."

"Sometimes, a change of scenery is all we need, right?"

Fern nodded. She agreed with Elliot, although she didn't add that sometimes, a change of scenery didn't help at all. She'd left Houston for a new place, and although the move had helped her in some ways, it hadn't done what she'd hoped for.

It hadn't erased the past.

"I'd love to paint it for you," she said. "I'll make sure it's ready for you before you leave."

The idea of Elliot leaving made Fern feel uneasy. She

didn't know why that was. After all, why shouldn't Elliot go and start a new life? She'd done it, and he deserved to start over, too.

But that meant she wouldn't see him again, and for some reason, pain stabbed her chest. She'd become quite fond of Elliot, and seeing him around the studio while they worked had become normal. She'd even come to expect Thatcher and Veronica to continue conjuring up ways to set them up. Although she knew the older couple didn't understand her life at all, or know why a relationship with Elliot wouldn't work, it was endearing that they tried so hard to give them a happily ever after.

"I know you're ready to start over," Fern said, thinking out loud. "But it doesn't always help to leave. Sometimes, it doesn't solve anything. Maybe it could be better if you stayed."

"It's not always that simple," Elliot said. "If it's terrible, I can always come back. Sometimes, it takes knowing what you lost before you know what you really want. Like the man who wrote that letter." He gestured toward the tin.

Fern nodded. "We can be so stubborn sometimes, huh?" She smiled.

"Too stubborn for our own good," Elliot agreed with a chuckle.

Fern looked up at him, and she was suddenly aware of how close they stood. He looked into her eyes, his hazel eyes dark, the golden flecks beautiful.

Her breath caught in her throat. She could smell his cologne, which was now clinging to her clothes. She waited for the fear to kick in, for the panic at being this close to him to trample her. It didn't come. Instead, they shared an amicable silence, smiling into each other's eyes.

Elliot leaned a little closer, and Fern knew he was going to close the distance and kiss her.

His phone rang, slicing through the silence between them.

He took out his phone and frowned when he saw who was calling. "This isn't good." He held the phone against his ear. "Tina? What's wrong?" He listened for a moment, his eyes filling with concern. "I'll be right there...no, no, don't even argue with me. I'm on my way." He hung up the phone. "I'm so sorry. My sister needs me."

"Of course, go," Fern urged. "I'll lock up."

"Thank you," Elliot said, hurrying past her and out the door.

Fern sighed and walked to the counter, picking up the tin Elliot had brought for her. It had been so sweet of him to think of her, and she was convinced that the letters were from the same people—the ones she'd found from the woman, and the ones he'd found from the man.

Maybe she would talk to Thatcher after all and see if she could find the answer to the burning question inside her—had those two people found their happiness? Or had they been forced to live without each other, no matter how strong their love had been?

After checking that everything was in order at the store so Linda could get right into admin the next morning, Fern locked up the shop and got into her car. She considered going to the studio apartment to finish the cleaning, but it was getting late, and she was tired. Cleaning the apartment was taking a lot longer than she'd thought it would, and she'd extended her stay at the Airbnb so that she could take care of everything. The lady who owned the property was now planning to be out of town for much longer than she'd thought, so she'd been happy to hear Fern wanted to stay on.

On the way back, Fern dialed her mother's number. The call reverberated through her car over the Bluetooth connection.

"Fernanda?" her mom said when she answered the phone. "My *carina,* how are you? I miss you."

"I'm doing well, *Mamá*," Fern said with a smile. "I miss you, too. How are things going?"

"Yes! Very well!"

Rosita gushed about something, but Fern didn't listen to the words her mother spoke. Instead, she listened closely to the way she said her words. Rosita was slurring her words a little, and her tone was forced. She was trying to sound happy.

"*Mamá,* are you alright?" Fern asked. "What's wrong?"

"Perfect, Fernanda, I'm perfect. You know me. I'm fine, I'm fine."

The more Rosita repeated herself, the more Fern worried. Her mother sounded almost hysterical.

"Where's Hank, Mom?" Fern asked. "Is he there?"

"He's out with his friends. He likes to go out, you know how he is."

Fern nodded, knowing exactly how Hank could be. He would stay at a pub all night long, drinking and blowing all their money, while Rosita was at home struggling with her mental health.

"Please call Dr. Kirkland, *Mamá*. Let him just look at you."

Rosita protested a few times, but Fern remained adamant until Rosita promised that she would call, if nothing else. Fern knew Dr. Kirkland would hear what she'd heard and determine if something needed to be done.

After talking to her mother a little longer, Fern ended the call. She had a hollow feeling in her stomach. Her mother needed her, and she was hours away from Houston. She couldn't be there for her mother.

"This is what you were looking for," she said, trying to convince herself. "You wanted to get away from the burden of that responsibility. You wanted your freedom, and now you have it."

Until now, the freedom had been incredible, and Fern had

never felt as alive as she did now that she was a part of so many different projects. But knowing that her mother might need her made her uneasy. What if something happened, and Hank wasn't there to look after Rosita?

Fern pushed away the thought. She couldn't keep being there for her mother, not when leaving had been all she'd wanted in the first place. She'd decided, taken a leap of faith, and had to trust that in the long run, everything would work out right.

She just had to keep pushing through. Being her own person without having to be the pillar of strength for everyone around her was a new sensation. She just had to keep moving forward until it was her new normal.

Everything was going to be fine.

Fern just hoped that was true and that she hadn't made a huge mistake by putting her mother in danger when she'd left.

# Chapter 14
# Elliot

Elliot floored it all the way to Rockport, breaking a lot of traffic rules as he did. In the back of his mind, he knew it was unreasonable to be this frantic. He didn't have to speed like the devil to get to his sister. She'd said she was okay and that there wasn't any imminent danger.

For so long, she'd been with a man who'd hurt her, and Elliot had felt so useless after he'd first learned about it. He hadn't known what pain she'd been going through, and it had caused him just as much pain knowing he hadn't been able to protect her from the hell her ex-husband had rained down on her again and again.

He just wanted to make sure she was okay. She'd been crying on the phone, and that had sent him into overdrive.

He flew through Rockport when he arrived, following the road he'd driven a million times before, and skidded into Tina's driveway with squealing tires.

"Tina!" he cried out before hammering his fist on the front door.

When the door opened, it revealed Tina with swollen eyes and a red nose.

"What happened?" he demanded. "Are you okay?"

"I'm okay," she said. "Elli, calm down. There's nothing wrong right now. I just..." Her voice caught in her throat, and she burst into tears again.

Elliot stepped forward and wrapped his arms around his sister, letting her sob against his chest. He realized that he didn't need to punch away anything, so his attention turned to his sister's emotional needs.

"How about we get a cup of tea and talk this through?" he suggested.

Tina nodded against his chest and sniffed. "Tea sounds good."

He followed her into the house, shutting the door behind him. In the kitchen, Tina filled the kettle and heated it up on the stove. Despite everything she'd been through, the kitchen was spotless. Her whole house was like that.

Elliot was glad to see that even though she'd been through something terrible, and there were still days when she struggled to get out of bed, she was on top of her life. She didn't let herself go, didn't let the house go—she kept living. She still went to work every day, although she'd initially been terrified of setting foot outside the door.

It took a very strong woman to do what Tina had done, and Elliot couldn't be prouder of her.

They made small talk while they waited for the kettle to boil. Tina seemed to want to skirt around whatever had made her cry. Elliot would let her avoid the topic for a while longer so she could use the time pulling herself together.

The kettle whistled, and Tina brewed two cups of tea. She added a lot of sugar to hers and milk into both before handing a cup to Elliot. Together, they walked to the living room, sitting down with their hot cups of tea.

"Talk to me, sis," Elliot said gently. It was time to unpack what was going on. "You know I'm here for you, no matter what."

"I know," Tina said. "It's why I called you. I got a call from Christopher today."

"What?!" Elliot roared, and a wave of fury raced through his body. Christopher was Tina's ex-husband. "Did you call the police?" Tina had a restraining order against him.

"No," Tina said, shaking her head. Her eyes filled with tears, and she sipped her tea, glancing at Elliot over the rim of her cup.

"Why not?" Elliot demanded. "If I catch that man, I swear—"

"He tried to apologize," Tina said, cutting him off.

Elliot frowned. "What?"

That didn't sound right. Christopher had been a menace. Not only had he hurt Tina—a lot—but he'd always made it sound like it was her fault that he'd done it. By the time Elliot had managed to get Tina out of the situation and away from that scumbag, she'd been convinced that he'd hurt her because something was wrong with her and not because Christopher was a monster.

"I know. I was shocked, too," Tina said, wiping tears from her cheeks with her sleeve. "But apparently, he's been going to some therapy thing for his anger, and one of the steps is to apologize to his victims, to ask their forgiveness."

Elliot bristled. He didn't want to accept that Christopher was doing something nice. "Was that all he said?" he asked suspiciously.

Tina nodded. "He told me he was sorry, that he knows he hurt me and that it wasn't on me, it's on him. He asked for my forgiveness."

"What did you say to him?" Elliot asked.

Tina shrugged. "The truth. I told him I would have to give

it time, that it would take a long time for me to get to a point where I could look back at what he did and be okay with it."

Elliot nodded slowly. He wanted to say all kinds of nasty things about Tina's ex-husband. He wanted to flip out and lose his temper that Christopher had called at all. Why couldn't he just let Tina move on with her life? Her life was hard enough as it was without the added complications of him reaching out to her again.

But Elliot didn't say anything. Instead, he kept his mouth shut and let Tina talk. It was the only way she could get things off her chest. Elliot was the only person who knew what she'd been through and who cared enough to listen. Their parents were there for Tina, but not in the way she needed at times. Elliot understood her emotions and would let her cry for hours. He would let her talk, or he would distract her from it all—whatever she needed to be okay.

His parents would never have done that for her. Just because Christopher was no longer in the picture didn't mean that all of Tina's problems had vanished.

"It was nice of him to call," Tina said.

Elliot bristled at that but said nothing.

"I appreciate that he's trying, I guess," she continued. "But he needs to know that I can't just forgive him like nothing happened. I still struggle with so many things, thanks to him. And I'm such an emotional mess all over again." Fresh tears ran down her cheeks. She tried to wipe them away, but when they came faster and faster, she gave up and sobbed. "It just brought everything back again. Hearing his voice sent chills down my spine and the fear came back, the terror. I was so scared something would go wrong, and the first thing I thought was, what did I do wrong?" She cried even harder. "I'm still there. I'm still stuck in this space where I blame myself, and I don't know how to get out of it."

Elliot pulled his sister against him, rubbing her shoulder while she wept. "It will just take time," he said.

"How much time will it take?" Tina asked through her tears. "It's been two years since we split up, one and a half since the actual divorce. I thought I would be okay by now."

"There's nothing wrong with taking your time. It's a big thing."

Tina nodded, and Elliot let her cry it out. He was just there for her, holding her, letting her work through her difficulties.

His mind wandered to Fern and how she'd reacted when she'd thought he was someone else. What exactly had she been through? Would she ever let him get close enough to be there for her the way he was for his sister?

The thought jolted through him. He hadn't realized he wanted to be there for Fern. Why did he feel this way? He'd told himself over and over not to get attached to her. But something about Fern drew him, and he couldn't deny it. He couldn't stop it. And he wished he could protect her the way he could his sister.

Fern looked like she needed someone in her corner.

Tina looked up at Elliot and wiped her tears for the final time. She'd stopped crying and already looked lighter now that she'd let everything out.

"Thank you for being here," she said. "It means a lot to me."

"Always, sis," Elliot said. "I'll always be here."

"You're such a great guy."

Elliot hugged her before she excused herself to freshen up. Once she left the room, Elliot looked out of the window at the night sky. The stars were bright outside, and when he strained his ears, he could hear the waves crashing on the beach that was not far from where Tina lived.

Could he afford to leave Tina behind if she needed him

this much? He'd told himself that it had been long enough since the divorce and convinced himself that she would be okay. But if this was what she still looked like...

"Are you okay?" Tina asked, walking back into the room.

She looked brighter and fresher now that she'd washed her face, and her eyes sparkled again. When she'd been married to Christopher, that light had dimmed. Elliot shuddered to think what might have happened if the abuse had gone on long enough that her light had been snuffed out completely.

"I'm fine," Elliot said. "I'm just glad you called me. I don't know if I should go."

"Go?" Tina asked, confused. "You can stay the night."

"No, I mean leaving for good. I don't know if it's a good idea. What if you need me, and I can't just speed from the next town over and be at your door in no time?"

Tina's face softened. "You need to get out of here, Elli. You need to do what you need to do. I get it, and I'm going to be okay. I'll call you. We can video call, too. We can make this work. And Mom and Dad are close by in case I really need help, you know."

Elliot nodded. His parents were there, and they could be there for Tina. They would help her out with whatever she needed; he knew that. But he still worried about her emotional well-being. Tina couldn't lean on their parents emotionally the way she leaned on Elliot. They just didn't understand. His mother was so caught up in her own melodrama that she seemed to forget other people had emotions and tough times. And his father...the man was a very cold, distant person. He'd been like that since the beginning, but as time had dragged on and his parents' marriage had fallen apart, with them drifting away more and more, it was as if his father had become colder and colder.

Neither of them looked after Tina the way Elliot felt she needed.

"I'm just worried about you," he finally said. The words were a very broad summary of what he felt about her situation, but they were enough.

"I know, but it's not your job to protect me, you know. You deserve to spread your wings and fly."

Elliot nodded. He knew his stubborn sister wouldn't suddenly tell him he needed to stay because she couldn't be without him. And she was right—he did deserve to do something like this.

The only problem was that the more he tried to cut himself loose from the small coastal town where he'd grown up and think about living in a big city, the more it seemed his roots had become firmly settled.

They talked a while longer, their conversation changing to lighter topics. It was after midnight when they finally got up and got ready for bed.

After making sure Tina was alright, Elliot walked to the spare bedroom where he'd stayed so many times before. He had some spare clothing in the closet, and he stripped to his boxers before getting between the sheets.

He let out a breath and closed his eyes, but sleep wouldn't come. Fern's face flashed before him, and it was all he could think about. He saw the way she laughed, the way she smiled. He could hear her voice in his mind. She had been so excited about the tin he'd given her, opening one of the letters and reading it with him. She was so passionate about her art, and everything she was passionate about became his passion, too. She was contagious in so many ways.

*What's going on with me? I can't get this involved with her. She is just another person working on the property where I am doing a job.*

But Elliot knew it wasn't that simple. Fern wasn't just another person who happened to be around. In the short time he'd gotten to know her, he had become truly fond of her. He was curious about her past and wished he could do something to help her; he was a helper by nature. It was why he felt so reluctant to leave Tina behind, too.

But he had so much on his plate, he couldn't afford to take on someone else. It wasn't his job, just like Tina had said.

He just had to keep reminding himself of that.

He closed his eyes and focused on clearing his mind so he could finally fall asleep. But when he did, Fern's face didn't disappear. Instead, she filled his dreams.

The next morning, Tina was already up by the time Elliot got out of bed. He heard her in the kitchen making breakfast. Elliot smelled coffee, and the aroma drew him to the kitchen.

"Morning," Tina said. She looked bright and cheerful; a lot better than last night. Elliot was relieved to see it.

"That smells so good," he said when Tina opened the oven door to check on the bacon.

"The least I can do for your efforts to console me is make you a hearty breakfast." Tina smiled happily.

Elliot grinned. He loved seeing his sister like this, back to her old self. The further she moved away from the terrible marriage she'd been stuck in, the more she regained parts of herself.

It was always so good to see.

"Tell me about your job in Waterstead," Tina said. "I want to know all about it. What are your clients like?"

"They're really great, actually," Elliot said, sipping the coffee his sister had put in front of him. "I didn't expect to find people I would want to be friends with."

"That does sound great," Tina said. "I'm so glad you're making friends."

Elliot shook his head, about to remind her that he was leaving, but he wasn't ready to get into that. Instead, he told her about working for Thatcher and Veronica and all the different projects they wanted him to take care of.

"It sounds like a lot of work still needs to be done," Tina said. "How long are you planning on being there?"

"Until it's done, I guess," Elliot said. "I still haven't found a place or decided where exactly I'm going, so I don't have a timeline yet."

Tina nodded thoughtfully. "Who's Fern?" she asked suddenly.

Elliot frowned. "Who?" Had he mentioned something to his sister?

"The woman who works for Veronica. You keep talking about her."

"Do I?" Elliot scratched his head, taking another sip of coffee. "Maybe it's because she's around all the time. We work in the same space."

"Sure," Tina said. "I get that she must be around. But you don't talk about her like she's just an ornament. Do you spend a lot of time together?" Her eyes sparkled.

"We spend a bit of time outside of work, yeah," Elliot admitted. "Veronica and Thatcher are determined to set us up, so we have dinners sometimes, the four of us. Fern also helped me with the boxes I wanted to donate."

"That's interesting," Tina said with a smirk.

"I know what you're thinking, and it's nothing like that," Elliot said, a smile playing around his mouth. He knew his sister would take an interest in what was happening between him and Fern—it seemed to be what everyone was interested in these days. "I am not looking for anything serious. I'm moving, remember?"

Tina shrugged. She sipped her coffee, her eyes dancing with laughter over the rim of her cup. "Maybe something can persuade you to stay." She waggled her eyebrows at Elliot, and he burst out laughing.

"I am serious—it's nothing like that. We are just good friends." He wasn't going to add that he was inexplicably attracted to Fern and didn't know why he felt so protective of her. Maybe it was just his protective instincts spilling over after being so invested in his sister's well-being. That had to be it, right?

Thankfully, the conversation turned in a different direction while they ate their breakfast, and finally, it was time for Elliot to leave. He hugged his sister.

"Promise me you'll call me if you need me," he said.

"You know I will," Tina said. "But I'm okay."

Elliot knew his sister would be okay, but he would never stop caring about her safety.

After he left her house, he drove to his warehouse in town. There, he loaded a couple of supplies into the back of his truck to take back to Waterstead.

As he drove back to the small waterside town, he felt a rush of excitement at seeing Fern again. He squashed the feeling as soon as it came—he couldn't allow himself to feel this way.

But still, the feelings crept back.

# Chapter 15
# Fern

After a long day at the studio, and an evening working in the studio apartment to make it livable, Fern drove to the Airbnb to have a quiet night at home. She was exhausted after working so hard on the studio apartment, and being on her feet every day at Veronica's studio was also taxing. She knew she would get used to it eventually, but it would take time.

And it was time Fern was more than happy to give. Veronica was a wonderful employer, and Fern was happier here than she had ever thought she could be. Her new job here, her new home in the small town, had been so much more rewarding than she'd expected.

And it had come with surprises, too.

Her mind was filled with thoughts of Elliot. She hadn't seen him the whole day—he'd left Linda's shop in a hurry to take care of his sister, and he'd been gone ever since. Fern had hoped he would swing by so she could ask him if everything was alright, but she didn't want to bother him. He clearly had his hands full, and she didn't want to make an unnecessary nuisance of herself.

She felt a strange attraction to Elliot, but she didn't want to assume he felt the same about her, even when the two of them shared something special. When she had first met Elliot, she had thought he was going to be a pain in her neck. But the more she got to know him, the more she realized he was a wonderful man.

She couldn't stop thinking about him.

Fern hoped that Elliot's sister would be okay. He had seemed so worried when he'd left the shop in a hurry. What was going on there? She was curious. Not because she was nosy, but because she wanted to be there for Elliot when he was in a state. And he'd seemed to be in a very bad state after his sister had called.

Why did she feel this way about Elliot? Why did she care so much about his emotions and what was going on in his life?

Fern knew the answer to that question. Elliot was very different from what she had originally assumed, and she was starting to like that person. When he wasn't trying to put on a face, and when he wasn't uncomfortable around Thatcher and Veronica and their matchmaking attempts, she saw a side of him that was very sweet. He'd opened up to her more, and she liked what she'd learned.

It was almost like she saw something secret about him, a part that he didn't show anyone else.

That she felt she could confide in Elliot in return was something that caught her off-guard. Fern had never felt like she could trust a man. A lot of that had to do with Hank—he'd never been someone she could turn to. In fact, she always felt like she should run away from him.

Even after she was old enough to know that not all men were like Hank, she'd hit a wall. Derek hadn't been abusive, but the relationship hadn't worked, partially because she could never trust him fully.

A lot of other things had come into play, too, but trust was a big thing in her life.

With Elliot, everything was different. He had a trustworthy way about him, and even though she was still scared, that was her past catching up with her, not something he did. She wished she could tell him those things—what her life had been like, and why she reacted that way toward him sometimes.

When she'd attacked him with the umbrella, she'd seen how much her emotional reaction had affected him. He was sensitive to things like that. She had felt bad about it, but it had been too much for her to deal with at the time.

Now, she wondered if she should try explaining it to him.

"Why would he care about your past, Fern?" she asked herself out loud. "He is leaving soon, and you'll never see him again. There is no use burdening him with things that have nothing to do with him."

She nodded at herself, confirming her words. She was just being silly, caught up in the emotions that the letters had stirred within her, swept away by Elliot's kindness in bringing her the letter he knew she would be interested in. She had to be careful and guard her heart. He wasn't going to be around here for very long, and she couldn't afford to get so attached to him.

Fern tried to decide what to do with her time. She thought about running a bath, reading a book, or doing something else that would allow her to relax. But her mind kept spinning into a hurricane of warring emotions.

When she felt like this, she usually painted. Getting out whatever she was feeling on canvas cleared her mind better than any therapy.

She left the Airbnb and walked to her car, finding her canvas and acrylic paint in the trunk. She carried her loot back to her room and set it up, turning on various lights and moving the bedside lamp to make sure the right light fell on her canvas. She took out her palette and mixed different colors before she let her brush do the talking. As she painted, she poured everything she felt into the picture. She switched her brushes, letting the colors come together. She breathed life into the canvas and got lost in the sensation of creating.

Whenever anything went wrong in her life, painting had been her escape. It was like meeting up with an old friend.

Hours passed. Fern mixed colors, layered them onto the canvas, and created a painting that would relish in its own existence. As she painted, her emotions calmed, and she felt like she could breathe again. Everything disappeared—her mom and Hank, the difficulties of deciding to move to a new place, the past that haunted her. All that mattered was the brush, its movement on the canvas, and the colors that came together in all the right ways.

Finally, when she sat back to study her handiwork, she gasped.

She had painted an incredible scene of the coast. The dark clouds above carried the hint of a storm building, and the waves were choppy because of the growing wind. The trees were brightly colored with evergreens, and the sky between the clouds was an impossible blue. When she looked at the painting, she felt like she could escape into it.

This was what Elliot had asked for when he'd asked her to do a painting for him. She hadn't set out to paint something for a commission—she'd only done it to escape. But this was a masterpiece, and she wanted him to take it with him. It was the perfect embodiment of what her life was like here in Waterstead. It wasn't his life, of course, but she believed it carried the raw emotion he was looking for. The idea that they could share something so personal, so intimate, made her feel it was right that Elliot have this painting.

She propped the painting against her closet door so it

would dry properly, then put her paints away before donning pajamas and climbing into bed. She fell back onto the pillows with a sigh, pushed her hands into her hair, and let her arms fall to the side. She felt so much better now that she had gotten everything out of her system.

When she closed her eyes, she thought about M and P, the two people who had somehow lost each other. It was so sweet and heartfelt to read their letters, and their pain was so real, she couldn't shake the thought of them.

Fern wished she could figure out what had happened to them. It seemed that they had understood love. If they had lost the true love they clearly felt for each other, it would be heartbreaking. Knowing their story was in the past and whatever had happened was already set in stone only made it that much sadder. Fern truly hoped that they had found their happy ending.

Finally, she fell asleep.

*The night was pitch black, the dark clouds blocking out the moon and stars. The wind tugged at Fern's clothes and hair, and she struggled to keep her balance as the wind pushed at her, whipping her back and forth. The waves were angry next to her, crashing down onto the sand with a vengeance, so loud that she could barely hear herself think.*

*A dark figure in the distance loomed.*

*"Hello?" Fern called out.*

*"Where have you been, Fern?" Hank growled, and somehow, his voice was perfectly audible above the sound of the impending storm. "I've been looking for you everywhere. Do you have any idea what you've done?!"*

*"I'm sorry!" Fern cried out, but the wind blew her words away.*

*"You're coming with me right now," Hank said. "We are going home. Your mother needs you, and I am done looking after her. She is nothing but a waste of my time."*

*He was suddenly right in front of Fern. There was nowhere to run, and she screamed. He grabbed her by the arms and shook her so hard, she thought her head would pop off her shoulders.*

Fern jerked upright in bed, breathing hard. Her hairline was wet with sweat, and she struggled to get herself under control.

"It was just a nightmare," she told herself, but it was difficult to shake the fear of Hank finding her. It twisted in her stomach and made her feel sick.

She couldn't go back to sleep; she was too worked up. She couldn't stay in the house, either—she had to get out. She had to see the world for what it was, not what her dream had conjured it to be.

Hank wasn't here. He didn't know where she was. She had been right to escape him.

She got up and got dressed, wrapping herself in warm clothes. During the day, it was hot, but at night, cold came across the water. She knew she would freeze if she left the house not wearing enough.

She climbed into her car and drove to the beach. The public beach was deserted, and Fern got out. She walked with her toes in the sand, carrying her shoes in one hand.

She could see Thatcher's and Veronica's house in the distance and used it as an anchor—a lighthouse of sorts. She wouldn't go that far, but the sight of it made her feel safer somehow. They were close by, people who cared for her. Fern fought to keep a grip on reality and not allow the nightmare to take over. All the while, fear rested on the edge of her consciousness.

While she walked, she tried to imagine something positive, something beautiful. Last night, she had painted a wonderful piece, so she tried to recapture the excitement she'd felt. But the nightmare had shaken her to her core, and it was difficult to feel anything other than panic.

A dark shadow on the horizon caught her attention, and Fern froze. For a moment, she was back in her dream, with Hank waiting for her. Fern knew this person couldn't really be Hank, and when she forced herself to take another step or two closer, she saw it was Elliot.

She wanted to go to him. She'd missed him after he'd left to go to his sister, and she hadn't seen him the whole next day. But now, he looked so much like Hank, she struggled to discern reality.

She was feeling just like she had when Elliot and Thatcher had come to the studio apartment that first day and she'd thought Hank was coming for her. And just like when she'd attacked Elliot with the umbrella.

She kept seeing Hank—fearing Hank—wherever she went.

She couldn't keep doing this. It wasn't fair to Elliot to keep seeing him as the bad guy just because of what someone else had done to her.

How long would she still have to face this fear?

Elliot lifted his hand and waved at her, looking happy to see her. Fern wanted to go to him, trying to convince herself it would be okay. But what would it mean? She knew she was starting to fall for Elliot. And then? He was leaving soon. And even if he wasn't...she was not the kind of person who could be with a man like him. She couldn't be with any man; no one would get a normal relationship with her. She was too battered, too emotional, and her past was still too fresh in her mind. She liked Elliot a lot, but she didn't want to pull him down just because she was struggling with her demons. He deserved so much more.

Wasn't that what love was about? Wasn't it about making choices with the other person in mind? If Elliot decided he wanted to be with her, she didn't have anything good to offer him. She was a mess more often than not.

Elliot took a couple of steps toward her, but Fern shook her head, and instead of going to him, she turned away.

She could barely see the road through the blur of her tears as she drove back to the Airbnb. Her heart broke, not only because she had turned away from someone she was falling in love with, but because she knew what she had to do.

When she walked into the room, she started to pack her things. Coming here had been a mistake. It had only shown her what she could never have. She should never have left Houston. You didn't miss what you didn't know.

Now that she knew what happiness could be like, she would forever miss it. But she wasn't the type of person someone like Elliot could take a risk with. She couldn't allow him to spend more time with her, to give her thoughtful gifts. Even if he didn't feel about her the way she felt about him, it still wasn't fair to him. She would always have a reaction that he never intended her to have. She would always be scared of him when he wasn't someone she should fear.

After packing her bags and loading them into her trunk, she sent a text to Veronica.

*I had to go home—I'll call. I'm sorry for leaving you like this.*

*F.*

It was ironic that she'd ended her note that way, Fern thought, but she put her phone away and walked to her car. She turned the ignition, the car coming to life in the chilly morning air, and she turned her car toward the main road that would take her away from Waterstead and back to the life she thought she'd left behind for good.

# Chapter 16
# Elliot

Elliot stood on the beach, staring at Fern's form as she ran away from him. He'd wanted to go to her, but something was bothering her. He'd seen it with her before—Fern had a past that kept coming back to haunt her at times when she least expected it, taking over when she was doing other things.

Maybe something like that had happened again. After seeing Tina, Elliot had stopped believing that Fern had something personal against him. They were forming a close friendship, a connection that meant more than whatever she feared. Fern's emotional reactions didn't necessarily mean that Elliot had done something wrong, only that a memory had been triggered by something he'd done.

He'd resolved never to scare Fern, to be careful with her, but there were things he couldn't help, and he was under the impression it had been one of those things again.

Elliot let out a deep breath and turned toward the water. He hadn't been able to sleep at the hotel after he'd spent some time working on smaller projects at the beach house, so he'd come out here to take in the fresh air, to try to clear his head.

He was no longer sure that leaving was the right thing to do. His sister needed him. Tina might have insisted she would be fine, but Elliot wasn't so sure after what had happened the night before. He also wasn't sure leaving was the right thing to do when he felt so attached to Waterstead and the people he'd met there.

Getting away from the life he lived here was what he wanted, though. Getting away from his parents' long-faded love and the small life he felt stuck in was the only way Elliot thought he could break free.

Lately, though, he'd started wondering about that. Was moving away really the answer? Would his worries about a loveless life follow him, and would his efforts to start over be in vain?

What if he moved to a small town like Waterstead to find purpose again?

It was these thoughts that had his head spinning, driving him out to the waterside in the early morning hours.

As dawn crept closer, the world around him changed. The monochromatic shades of the night bled away, replaced by splashes of orange and pink. The sky transformed, and the world burst into color and life, welcoming another day.

Elliot watched as the sun peeked its blood-red head over the horizon and slowly rose into the sky. The world sang, touched with hues of orange. The new dawn injected color into the world again, and the morning was beautiful, bursting with the pride of its mere existence.

Elliot took a deep breath and let it out slowly. Out here, he could breathe, he could think. Out here, he could *live*.

When the sunrise's orchestra of color and light subsided as the sun rose higher into the sky, he turned away from the ocean and walked back into town. The town was still asleep. Elliot enjoyed the quiet of the morning.

His mind drifted back to Fern. He wanted to reach out to

her and make sure she was okay. The protector in him wanted to chase away whatever was bothering her and fight all her demons. If she'd been through anything like what his sister had been through—and he was sure she had—he wanted to help her, to be there for her. He knew how tough it could be to navigate the world alone after a history of abuse, and everyone needed someone in their corner.

With his experience with Tina, though, Elliot also knew that as much as victims needed support, they sometimes wanted to process and heal on their own. Tina had often pushed him away when she'd struggled with something, working things out in her mind that he couldn't help with. No doubt, if Fern had been through the same ordeal in one way or another, she had the same difficulties sometimes and needed her space to figure out how to move forward.

Elliot didn't know where she stood now. He didn't know if she needed him to go to her and be there for her, or if he needed to leave her alone so she could have space. He also didn't know how to find out what she needed. As close as he felt to her sometimes, as deep as their connection went, he also didn't want to impose. They were closely connected in some ways, as if they'd always known each other, but they were strangers in other ways. He didn't want to butt in where it might be inappropriate.

He finally reached the hotel as the first people in town crept out of their homes. He walked up to his room and shut himself in. He collapsed onto the bed, exhaustion finally catching up with him. When he glanced at the time, he figured he could take a few hours to sleep before meeting with Thatcher.

He sent Thatcher a text, explaining he would be a little late after a rough night.

*Take your time, get your rest. I'll see you later,* Thatcher replied almost immediately.

Elliot smiled, put his phone on mute, and lay back on the bed. Thatcher and Veronica were wonderful people. Sure, they could be a little pushy sometimes—and a little nosy, prying into his business when Elliot was used to being a closed book —but they genuinely cared about him and Fern. People like them were hard to come by.

When he'd first met them, he'd felt uncomfortable around them. Their relationship had reminded him of his parents, of their marriage that had dried up and become a façade. But as he'd gotten to know them better, he'd realized they were nothing like the people who'd raised him. Not only did they seem to care for each other deeply in a way that would never fade, that same affection spilled onto everyone around them, and Elliot had been a happy recipient of their attentiveness.

Thatcher and Veronica were one of the reasons Elliot wasn't so sure he wanted to move away anymore.

He closed his eyes, pushing those thoughts from his mind so he could try to get a few hours' sleep before working again.

When he opened his eyes, the sun was high in the sky. He picked up his phone and noticed it was almost eleven in the morning. He'd slept a good few hours, and although his nap hadn't been a full night's sleep, he felt better. He was energized and ready to go.

His phone showed no messages from Fern, and his heart sank a little. He would see her a bit later and talk to her, he decided. His phone also showed a missed call from Michelle, the realtor.

His stomach twisted, but he called her back.

"Elliot, how are you?" she answered almost immediately, and he could hear the smile in her voice.

"I'm doing just fine," he answered, thinking how ironic it was that those words were true. He *was* doing just fine, right here where he was.

"Have you had a chance to check your email? I sent you a few options to consider."

"I haven't had a chance to check yet," Elliot admitted.

"Not to worry. Have a look and let me know what you think. As soon as you decide which you like, we can go ahead and schedule a viewing."

"Michelle, I don't—"

"Oh, I'm so sorry to cut you off, but I have to go. Have a look and call me—we'll talk then." She ended the call abruptly.

Elliot still had the words in his mouth. *I'm not sure moving is the right thing to do anymore.*

He shook his head and opened the email app on his phone. She'd sent an email with a few links to different homes. He didn't click on any of them. He would do it when he had time, and he would consider everything one more time. He had to really think about what it would all mean—what it would be like if he packed everything up and left, and what it would be like if he stayed.

He closed his email app, walked to the bathroom to take a quick shower, and headed out to Thatcher's place.

The beach house looked so much better now that Elliot had finished some of the projects. He'd sanded and varnished some floors, fixed several of the broken window frames, and replaced three bedroom ceilings.

Today, he worked in the kitchen, replacing the broken cabinet doors and sanding and varnishing the rest. Buster lay nearby, his tongue lolling as he slept. Elliot liked the company —during his time here, he'd become fond of even the dog. Buster was a character, and if Elliot left, he would miss him as much as he would miss everyone else.

He whistled while he worked, his mind wandering in all directions, trying to decide what he should do about staying or going.

Thatcher appeared at the door, watching Elliot varnish the doors for a while before Elliot realized he was there. When he looked up, Thatcher grinned at him.

"Coming along, huh?" Thatcher asked.

"Yeah, it looks like this will be an easier job than I thought," Elliot said, straightening. He stretched his back until it popped. "I think it's really coming together."

"It looks a lot better than I would have managed in this amount of time. I wouldn't have gotten around to most of this stuff. And the ceilings were a big one. As soon as we hit monsoon season, it will help that it's all been taken care of."

"It's always good to be prepared," Elliot said, rubbing his hands on his dusty jeans. "Is Veronica at the studio today?"

Thatcher nodded. Veronica had opted to work from home for a few days in an attempt, Elliot believed, to get him and Fern to spend more time together.

"Yeah, she left early this morning, saying she had a few things to take care of. She looked troubled."

"Is it anything serious?" Elliot asked with a frown.

Thatcher shrugged. "I don't know. I don't think so—Veronica would have said something if it was. I've learned to let things be. She'll tell me if it's something she wants me to know. Otherwise, I'm letting her live the way she needs to live. When people go through tough times, it's better to let them reach out for the help they need when they need it rather than trying to force it on them. Even with the best of our intentions, we can screw up sometimes."

Elliot nodded. "I know all about that." It only confirmed that he'd been right not to go after Fern when she'd run away from him that morning. They had a good relationship, and he trusted that when he next saw her, she would tell him what was going on—if that was what she needed.

"I have a few things I need to take care of at the studio,"

Elliot said. "These doors need to dry before we put the knobs and handles on again."

"That sounds good. I was just on my way out there, anyway. Come on, let's drive up together."

Elliot nodded.

Buster hoisted himself to his feet and accompanied them to their cars.

"You can't come with us, buddy," Thatcher said.

Buster whined and tried to get into Thatcher's truck anyway. Thatcher barred him with his knee, and finally, Buster gave up. He turned and headed for Elliot's truck, but Elliot closed the door quickly.

His window was open, and Buster jumped up, facing Elliot directly.

"We'll be back, big guy," Elliot said. "You look after the place, and we'll come back for you."

Buster sighed heavily, dropping himself to the ground as if he'd understood every word. He walked to his kennel and lay down with another sigh, putting his big head on his paws.

Elliot smiled at the dog and shook his head. It was crazy how an animal could play on his feelings so much, but Buster wasn't just any old animal. He was part of Thatcher's and Veronica's family, and he had become a friend to Elliot as much as they had.

Elliot put his truck in gear and followed Thatcher into town.

"Elliot, it's good to see you!" Veronica called out as the men walked into the studio. She walked to them from behind the front counter. "I thought you were coming to the studio again tomorrow."

"I'm waiting for the varnish in the kitchen to dry, so I figured I could finish up those cubbies in the back room while I wait."

"You're very efficient," Veronica said with a smile.

Elliot glanced around the studio, looking for Fern. He found he missed her, although he'd never say it out loud. He also wanted to make sure she was okay after their incident this morning.

She didn't seem to be around, though. He didn't want to ask Veronica where she was—Thatcher and Veronica were already under the impression that Elliot and Fern belonged together. He didn't know how they would react if they suspected their efforts were working.

"I'll be in the back room if you need me," Elliot finally said.

He walked to the back room and found it empty, too. Fern didn't seem to be in the studio at all. And judging by the lack of humming from the upstairs apartment, she wasn't up there cleaning, either.

It only worried him more that something was wrong. Why wasn't she here? If it had been a normal day, maybe he wouldn't have worried so much, but she'd had that panicked reaction this morning. He'd really hoped he could check on her. He knew from experience that everything felt worse during the night, and as soon as the light of day broke, what seemed terrible often wasn't that bad.

He hoped the same was true for her.

"She's fine," he muttered to himself. "She's probably just running errands for Veronica and will be back a bit later. Better to focus on work."

He worked on the cubbies, continuing what he'd started a few days ago. The cubbies had been measured out, the structures already erected. Today, he would add the doors so the cubbies could be closed, and the students could store their canvases in them after class with Fern.

He was pleased with how the cubbies looked so far. Fern would like them, and the idea made him smile.

"As soon as she comes back, I'll show her the cubbies, and

then we can talk about this morning," he told himself. "She'll be okay to talk about this morning, it's not like we're strangers anymore. Or maybe I should just call her. Friends can do that, right? I'll call her up and check that she's okay. Unless...what if that's not what she wants?" He groaned. "You're being an idiot."

"Who are you talking to?" Veronica asked, suddenly behind Elliot.

He jumped. "I didn't hear you come in," he said, scratching the back of his head. He felt like a fool talking to himself. He hadn't meant for Veronica to hear him; he'd thought she and Thatcher were still in the front.

"No, I imagine you didn't." A smile played around her lips. "You were in deep conversation."

Elliot felt his cheeks redden. "It was nothing. Sometimes I run through things out loud to get my thoughts straight. You know...to know what still needs to be done, what I shouldn't forget, stuff like that."

"Mental notes out loud?" Veronica asked.

Elliot nodded. "Yeah, something like that."

"You were talking about Fern, weren't you?" Veronica asked. "You're not sure if she's okay."

Elliot wasn't sure how much to say. How much did Veronica know about Fern's past?

"Well...she just looked a little out of it this morning when I saw her, so I thought—"

"You saw her?" Veronica asked, surprised.

Elliot nodded. "It was early, on the beach." He didn't know how to tell Veronica the rest. He could only speculate that she'd been running from something, but he didn't know what.

"I have to tell you something," Veronica said, glancing down at her hands. "Fern is gone."

"What?" Elliot asked, shocked.

Veronica nodded. "She left. She didn't even say goodbye, she just left me a text. Whatever her reasons, I think you might be right in thinking that something might be up. I tried to call her, but no answer."

Elliot stared at Veronica. Whatever had bothered Fern that morning had been enough to send her packing. What if she was in real danger?

"Where did she go?" Elliot asked.

"I don't know. Why don't you reach out to her? Maybe she'll open up to you more." Veronica put her hand on Elliot's arm affectionately before she left the back room without waiting for him to answer. It had only been a suggestion.

Elliot stood in the room, confused and worried.

At lunchtime, he convinced himself to call Fern, but her phone went straight to voicemail. His worry mounted.

When the day was over and Elliot had taken care of everything he could, he got into his truck, declining a dinner invitation from Thatcher and Veronica. Instead, he drove back to Rockport.

Tina opened the door with a frown when he parked in her driveway. "What a surprise to see you," she said.

Elliot nodded. "Usually, I come when you need me, but today, it's the other way around."

Tina smiled. "I'm glad you still think I'm someone you can lean on."

When Elliot reached her, he hugged her. "Of course. You're not your past and your difficulties, you're more than that. You've always been my best friend. We've been through a lot together."

"And I'll always be here for you," Tina said. "Come in."

In the kitchen, Tina made coffee while Elliot told her everything she didn't already know about Fern. He didn't leave anything out to spare Fern, wanting Tina to know the full picture.

When the coffee was ready, they walked to the living room and sat down in their usual seats.

"I don't know where she is now," he finally said after explaining what had happened that morning. "I don't know if I should reach out to her or try to find her. We're not that close, and we barely know each other. She didn't confide in me about any of these things. At this point, I'm speculating about what she might have gone through."

Tina nodded slowly. "But you think she needs help."

"I don't know. All I know is that I'm worried about her."

"Do you want to know what I think?" Tina asked.

"Of course, that's what I came here for."

"I think you should stop being so careful, throw caution to the wind, and go for it."

"Go for what?"

"For Fern. I'm not just talking about you reaching out to see if she's okay. I'm talking about the whole thing—be there for her, be with her, love her."

Elliot blinked at his sister. "I don't know if that's how I feel about her."

Tina groaned. "Come on. It's the most obvious thing in the world that you're in love with her."

Elliot frowned. Was that really what this was? But the more he thought about it, the more he realized his sister was right. He didn't only worry about Fern because he understood what she might be going through. He worried about her because he was in love with her. He cared a lot more for her than he'd thought possible.

"I don't know if I'm the right man for her," Elliot finally said. "I know what I feel—thanks to you—but I don't know her past. And I don't know if I'm someone who can help her, or someone she'll fear because of the demons she's fighting."

Tina took Elliot's hand. "That's exactly why you're the right man for her. You know how to be around her, and you understand what she's going through. Do you think any other man would have understood why she attacked you with an umbrella? Why you guys can laugh and laugh, and then it goes all wrong and she runs away from you? It's crazy if you don't understand how it works, but *you* understand. You've always been so understanding, and I think you were brought into each other's lives for that reason. I think you're meant to be together."

Elliot stared at his sister, turning her words over and over in his head. Could it be? Were he and Fern in each other's lives because they were right for each other? Or was it just coincidence?

The more he thought about it, the more he thought that maybe his sister was right. Why else would he have run into Thatcher and Veronica and be introduced to someone like Fern when he was about to make a decision that would change his life...possibly for the worse?

"I don't know what to do," Elliot admitted.

"I do," Tina said firmly. "Stop following your head and start listening to your heart."

Elliot nodded. He'd always been the guy to think things through, always being logical, working through everything step by step. That mindset wasn't going to work this time. If he followed those rules, he would end up moving, and Fern wouldn't be in his life.

He realized with striking clarity that he didn't want that.

# Chapter 17
# Fern

Being back home felt...strange. Fern woke up in her old bed, looking up at the ceiling she'd known her whole life. The house's sounds around her were familiar, but they weren't soothing.

Hank's sports channel was blaring so loudly, she couldn't sleep through it. She didn't hear her mom's off-tune humming accompanying the blasting TV, but maybe she was still sleeping.

Fern hoisted herself out of bed and looked at herself in the mirror. Sometimes, she didn't even recognize the woman staring back at her anymore. While living in Waterstead, Fern had felt alive in ways she never had before. Her art had flowed out of her with renewed creativity and passion, and she'd looked forward to a bright future for the first time in her life.

But it just wasn't that simple. In Waterstead, she'd felt out of her depth. She hadn't known the town or the people very well, who had all been so connected, so close to each other. She'd loved being a part of that, but she had to accept the facts: She didn't belong there.

She belonged here in Houston, where she could look after

her mother, where she would figure out some other way to do her art and bring in money.

Bitterness coated her tongue, but being back home wasn't a bad thing. She just had to keep reminding herself of that.

She picked up her hairbrush and pulled it through her hair, working her way through the tangles after a long night of restless sleep. In some ways, being home was a relief. She was back in a place she understood. She didn't necessarily like this life, but she understood it. The good and the bad times here were predictable, and that created some stability for her.

In Waterstead, Fern had felt on the verge of panic too many times, though there had been times when she'd felt at home, like she belonged. She would miss that, but she would hold onto the fact that she knew this life and its ins and outs. Even if they were bad. Rather the devil she knew than the devil she didn't.

The other reason she'd decided to come back—perhaps the biggest reason of all—was that here, she couldn't hurt the people she loved. Too many times in Waterstead, she had done things to the well-meaning people around her that they didn't deserve.

Who was she kidding? It wasn't *people*. It was just one person.

Elliot.

He deserved so much better than the erratic life she brought with her. He deserved more than the chaos she could offer.

When she'd seen him on the beach and couldn't shake the image of Hank hurting her, she'd run away from him. It had hurt him; she knew that. That was exactly why she'd decided to leave—she couldn't be anyone other than herself, and she couldn't keep hurting Elliot. He was too sweet, too nice. He was there for her in ways people had never been there for her, and she was terrified that she would never be good enough for him.

What if he decided not to follow through on his plans to move because of her? What if he wanted to be with her? She'd fallen in love with him, and she couldn't bring herself to rob him of happiness because the life she offered was filled with... crazy.

There, she'd said it. Fern didn't have the same mental challenges as her mother, but she knew she wasn't all there, not really. Not if she kept seeing the past. Not if her experiences haunted her so much, they became someone else's problem.

She knew she wasn't crazy, per se, but she was too close to it for comfort. The people she'd come to love—Elliot, and even Veronica and Thatcher—deserved someone who was collected and calm. Someone who could handle the challenges of life.

Fern's mind drifted to the students she'd signed for Veronica. She hated that she'd left her new friend in the lurch. Veronica would have to find a new art teacher, and she'd just prepared the classroom for Fern so she could start teaching.

Fern was sure Veronica would find someone much better suited for the job. She would keep telling herself that, and that would eventually override her guilt for leaving without even saying goodbye.

The thought made Fern sad, and she pushed it away. Instead, she walked to the bathroom and turned on the water to shower.

After an unpleasant, cold shower—she would have to check the heating in the house—she walked through the rest of the house. When she'd returned home, it had been so late, she'd snuck into the house and crawled into bed. She'd spent most of the day driving to Houston, trying to clear her head.

Now, in the new light of day, she got a fresh look at the

house. She was appalled at what she saw. In Fern's absence, the house had turned into a dump. Rubbish lay all over, with takeaway cartons covering every surface, empty beer bottles on the coffee table, and food crawling with maggots in the kitchen sink. The bin hadn't been taken out in days—it overflowed onto the tiles, and flies had gathered there to lay more eggs.

"*Mamá*?" Fern called.

No answer other than Hank's blaring television.

Fern shook her head, found rubber gloves under the sink, and started cleaning. She disposed of the old food in the sink and took out the trash. After the bin was available again, she moved through the kitchen and dining room, clearing up dirty plates, throwing away takeaway cartons, and getting rid of everything that made the house look like a dump.

Clearly, no one was taking care of the place. In her absence, everything had fallen apart.

Fern felt guilty for leaving. She'd thought her mother and Hank were adults, able to run their own lives, but that wasn't true. Rosita needed help, and her behavior could be erratic at times. She was the reason Fern had stayed and helped all these years, and if Rosita hadn't been able to run the home, she couldn't be blamed. Hank, on the other hand...

While Fern worked, she became more and more upset. How could Hank let them live in squalor like this? How could he not care? How could he let his partner live in a pigsty? Surely, there had to be a part of him that cared.

But Fern knew the answer to that—he didn't. The only person Hank had ever cared about was himself. He'd moved into their home, taken over their lives, and forced them to take care of him and themselves without ever lifting a finger to help.

Fern had tried to get out, but her mother hadn't been able to. Fern knew that no matter how much it hurt, this was where she had to be. She had to take care of her mom, who would never be able to take care of herself.

Only, now that she'd seen what life could be like—filled with color and light and love from people all around her—being back in the drab, loveless world she'd grown up in hurt that much more.

"I should never have left Houston," she muttered to herself.

"You're damn right you never should have left," Hank's gruff voice sounded from the kitchen door.

Fern spun around. Her heart beat in her throat, fear already in overdrive when she saw Hank's disgusting form. He wore a stained shirt and shorts that were torn on the sides, and his hair looked like it hadn't been combed in years. He had a couple of days' stubble on his chin. His mouth was twisted into a menacing snarl, and his eyes were cold and merciless.

"You have some nerve coming back here like nothing's changed."

"Nothing has changed," Fern pointed out. "This place is worse than ever. You couldn't clean up after yourself a bit? Where's my mom?"

"Who do you think you are, telling me what I should and shouldn't do in my own house?" Hank growled. He balled his meaty hands into fists.

A shiver traveled down Fern's spine, but she'd had enough of this. She'd seen that life could be better, and it was time things changed.

"This isn't your house, it's ours," Fern pointed out. "You didn't buy it, and you don't do anything to pay for it or maintain it. I'm the only one doing that. So, I'm the only one who gets to say what should and shouldn't happen around here."

Hank was suddenly furious. "Why, you little..."

He stomped into the kitchen, coming at Fern like a force

of nature. She backed up from him until her back hit the wall next to the fridge. He grabbed her upper arms, his fingers digging into her skin until she cried out.

"Don't you dare talk to me like that, do you hear?" He pinned her against the wall, his face right up against hers. "I won't tolerate your attitude. You want to stay here, you follow my rules. I want some respect."

Fern expected Hank to slam her against the wall, to shake her until it felt like her head would fall off.

He didn't.

He let go of her.

"This is your first and only warning," he said. "If you look for trouble again, you're going to find it."

He spun around and marched out of the kitchen. Fern's body had turned to jelly, and she sank toward the floor, shivering and whimpering.

"He didn't hurt me, he didn't hurt me," she muttered to herself, but it didn't matter. He might not have hurt her this time, but he'd hurt her before, and he would hurt her again. It was only a matter of time.

What else could she do besides submit to him, do as he wanted, and keep herself safe? Running away hadn't worked. Standing up to him hadn't worked. There was only one thing left to do.

After Fern pulled herself together again, she walked through the house to the master bedroom. There, everything was a mess, too. Clothes lay everywhere, and judging by the smell, washing hadn't been done in a while. She held her breath and pushed the bedroom door open.

"*Mamá?*" she said softly. "It's time to wake up."

Her mother wasn't in bed. The room was empty.

Fern frowned and searched the rest of the house before walking to the living room where Hank sat in front of the TV, drinking a bottle of beer. She hadn't had a chance to clean the living room and wouldn't until he was out of it.

"Where's my mom?" Fern asked.

Hank didn't answer.

"Hank?"

"What?" he bit out.

"Where's my mom?"

"Beats me," Hank said with a shrug. "Who knows what she gets up to these days."

"Is she in the hospital?"

Hank snorted. "You know she just does that for attention, right? No way I'm letting her get away with that anymore."

Fern shook her head, worry setting in. She left Hank to his TV and picked up the phone. She dialed Dr. Kirkland's personal number, and he answered after a few rings.

"I'm sorry to bother you, doctor," Fern said. "I just want to check in and hear if you've spoken to my mom recently."

"Not for a while," Dr. Kirkland said. "Is everything alright?"

"I hope so," Fern said, then she ended the call.

She was really starting to worry now. It was clear her mother was missing, and she didn't know where to start looking. Her mom could be anywhere, wandering the streets, not knowing who or where she was.

She dialed the police next. The police came over, and she told them everything she could. They said they would do what they could to find Rosita, but Fern worried more and more that nothing could be done. The police could only help so much.

Fern was an emotional mess. She'd come back home to find that everything was so much worse than she'd left it, and now the person she'd done everything for was missing.

In an attempt to finally live a life she could be proud of, Fern had left Rosita alone with Hank, and now she was gone.

Guilt washed over Fern in waves, so much so that she couldn't think straight. Her mind spun—she should never have left; she should never have tried to look for greener pastures. If she'd been here, her mother wouldn't have gone missing.

She wished she had a friend whose shoulder she could cry on. In Waterstead, she would have turned to Veronica, but after leaving her high and dry like that...would Veronica ever forgive her?

Tears welled up in Fern's eyes and spilled over her cheeks. Despite feeling like she'd failed everyone in her life, and fearing her new friends would never want to talk to her again, she dialed Veronica's number. Veronica had been one of the few people who had listened to her and been there for her, even when she'd known nothing about Fern.

Elliot had also been there for her, but she'd already burdened him with enough of her troubles. He didn't need any more of them from her.

"Fern," Veronica said when she answered the phone. "Oh, thank goodness, I've been worried sick about you."

"I'm sorry," Fern started before bursting into tears.

It took Veronica a while to calm Fern down enough that she could speak coherently.

"I should never have left," she cried. "I shouldn't have left my mom here. I should have stayed. I should have done the right thing. I just thought I could make a life for myself. I thought I deserved better."

"You do deserve better," Veronica said softly.

"I don't! Look at what's happened. No matter where I go, I ruin things. I don't make them better. I don't know what to do now. I'm so worried about my mom, and I have no idea where she might be. Will you keep an eye out for her?"

"How can I keep an eye out for her?" Veronica asked.

"I don't know. Maybe she tried to find me and went all the

way there. Maybe she's here somewhere..." Her voice caught in her throat, and she couldn't say the words.

"Okay," Veronica said after a moment. "I'll look out for her. I'll help where I can, okay?"

"Thank you. I don't deserve so much kindness from you after how I treated you—"

"Nonsense," Veronica said, cutting her off. "You deserve only the best, and we're always here for you. No matter what. Just because you have a difficult past and your life isn't smooth sailing doesn't mean you don't deserve support and love and friendship. And that's exactly what we plan to give to you."

The more Veronica talked, the more Fern wept. What had she done to deserve such wonderful, kind people in her life?

Despite everything going wrong, Fern felt a little better when she ended the call. She stood and walked into the house.

"What's for lunch?" Hank asked.

Fern frowned at him. "What?"

"Lunch. I'm hungry. What are you making?"

Fern shook her head in disgust. "Mom is missing, Hank. Do you remember that part?"

"She's all over the place. She'll turn up," Hank said, waving his hand in dismissal. "It's not the first time this has happened, and I doubt it will be the last."

Fern stared at him, her mouth agape. "What do you mean, it's happened before?"

"She's turned into quite the little wanderer since you left. Runs in the family, it looks like."

Fern gasped. "How long has she been gone before? How did you find her?"

"I told you, she comes back. So, about lunch..."

Something inside Fern snapped. "Mom is missing," she said in a clipped voice. "Don't you care at all?"

Hank rolled his eyes and groaned. "I heard you the first ten times."

That was it. Hank didn't care—he never had, and he never would. Fern was tired of tiptoeing around him and his moods.

"You're pathetic!" she shouted.

Hank stared at her, blinking.

"What did you just call me?"

"Did I stutter?" Fern snapped. "I said, you're pathetic. You're a grown man without the capacity to take care of yourself. You're a big bully, waiting for other people to create a life for you. You think you rule the roost, but without me and my mom, you're nothing. You have nothing. You haven't tried to amount to anything in your life, which means you have nothing to show for your existence, and I'm done."

"Done with what?" Hank seemed so shocked, he forgot to be angry and domineering.

"Done with you. As soon as I find Mom, we're out of here."

Hank opened his mouth to speak, but Fern wouldn't let him. It was liberating to get years' and years' worth of frustration off her chest. She wasn't even scared of him in that moment, although she probably would be once the adrenaline faded. But right then, she knew what she wanted—to go back to Waterstead and live a life without fear and pain and regret. She wanted her mother to be safe, and she wanted them to get away from Hank once and for all.

Her mom would love Waterstead. She would thrive there, and Fern vowed to take her back with her to the small town. Why hadn't she thought about it before? She could take care of Rosita and still live a good life.

She just had to find Rosita first.

A sickening feeling of dread filled Fern. What if they never found her mom? She shoved the thought away, refusing to think like that. She would try to stay positive. It was the only way forward.

When her phone rang, she grabbed it. She'd hoped it was

the police with good news, but Veronica's name flashed on the screen instead.

"Hello?" Fern asked, confused.

"She's here," Veronica said.

"What?"

"Your mom, she's here. You were right. I think she came looking for you."

"Oh!" Fern cried out, clapping her hand over her mouth. Her eyes welled with tears. "I'll be right there. I'm coming as fast as I can."

"She's safe, Fern. Drive safe—there isn't any danger."

Fern ended the call, grateful that things were working out okay. She ran back into the house and grabbed her still-packed bag.

"Where are you going?" Hank called out.

Fern ignored him. She felt strangely free now that she'd put him in his place. She didn't care what he thought—she didn't care about him at all—and he didn't deserve an explanation of any kind.

He didn't care, anyway.

She jumped into her car. Her other things were still in the trunk; she'd only taken out a bag of her clothes. Her tires squealed as she raced down the road.

She was going to find her mom and make sure that Rosita was always safe from now on. She was going back to Waterstead to create a new life.

She was going home.

# Chapter 18
# Elliot

Elliot had made up his mind—he was staying. Maybe not in Rockport, but he wasn't leaving to go to the city. He had half a mind to settle right here in Waterstead, in the little town that had bewitched him so.

"Are you sure this is what you want?" Michelle asked when Elliot called her to tell her he wouldn't be viewing any of her apartment options after all. "I know it's a big move, a big step to take, but moving to the city can be truly rewarding."

"I'm sure," Elliot said, nodding as he walked down the stairs to the hotel lobby. "I think I belong here. I can't leave just yet."

"Please, think about it a little more. Taking the leap is worth it in the long run, and it's not the kind of thing you want to give up on just like that. You've thought long and hard about it, and everyone gets cold feet when they think about a big change."

Elliot nodded even though Michelle couldn't see him. "I'm sure it's what I want. I'm sorry to cancel on you now after you've run around for me so much. It's the right thing to do for me."

Michelle was upset that Elliot wasn't moving, but he knew it wasn't personal. She would lose out on the commission of a sale. He felt bad that he'd sent her on a wild goose chase only to cancel on her now, but it was necessary.

After he'd talked to Tina last night, Elliot had made up his mind. He believed Fern had crossed his path for a reason, and he would do everything he could to be there for her. He didn't know if she would come back to Waterstead, but if she did, he would be here, waiting for her. Their story wasn't finished yet, even though she'd left. He felt it in his bones.

His mind wandered to the letters they'd read together, about the couple who'd been torn apart. Had they ever found their way back to each other? He hoped so—he hoped that the same would happen for him and Fern. In light of the letters, it was ironic that she'd left; he felt as lost without her as the people in the letters had seemed. The symbolism wasn't lost on him.

He parked his truck in front of V Studios and glanced up and down the road, looking for Fern's car. His heart sank a little when he didn't see it, although he'd told himself it wouldn't be there.

Still, he would never stop looking. He would always check to see if she was there. One day, he hoped she would be.

When Elliot pushed the door open, the cool blast of the air-conditioning welcomed him, but the studio was anything but peaceful. Veronica stood in the middle of the room, her hands out in supplication, looking up at a woman Elliot could only describe in one word—lost.

"Okay, Mrs. Cantu, it's okay," Veronica said, trying to keep her tone gentle, but she sounded pleading.

Elliot stopped and frowned at the scene before him. The woman with graying dark hair stood on a pedestal where a painting would be displayed, and she smiled and turned in a circle. The painting had been propped up against a wall.

"It's so good of you all to come," she said, waving her hand. "I didn't expect such a turnout."

Elliot glanced at Veronica and Thatcher, who stood a short distance away, scratching his head in confusion. He looked almost as lost as the woman on the pedestal, although she looked happy to be there. Thatcher looked like he'd rather be somewhere else.

"This place is beautiful! I love art," the woman continued. "My daughter does art, do you know?"

"She does wonderful art," Veronica said. "She created this display."

"Ah, my darling girl," the woman said warmly, beaming with pride.

Thatcher spotted Elliot and walked over to him.

"What's going on here?" Elliot asked in a low voice.

"Beats me," Thatcher said. "When I arrived here a couple of minutes ago, I found them like this. Veronica looks calm enough; she seems to know what's going on. This place is a magnet for strange people, let me tell you." He chuckled.

Elliot wasn't sure what to make of it. "Who is she?"

"Veronica said something about her being Fern's mother, but I haven't had a chance to ask more. She got onto that pedestal, and now I'm worried she'll fall and break something."

Elliot stared at the woman again. She had dark hair and bronze skin, so in that regard, she looked nothing like Fern with her auburn hair and pale skin. But in the structure of her face, her delicate nose and straight jawline, he could see Fern.

"How did she get here?" he asked.

Thatcher only shook his head.

"Please, Mrs. Cantu—" Veronica tried again.

"Rosita," the woman said. "Mrs. Cantu was my *Mamá*."

"Rosita, then," Veronica pleaded. "Will you get off the pedestal? Let's have a cup of tea and talk."

Rosita ignored her, turning around and around on the pedestal as if she was dancing rather than standing on a precarious structure. The pedestals were built for art, not for the weight of a woman, slight as this one may be.

The sound of a car pulling up interrupted Veronica, and she looked over her shoulder. Within seconds, Fern barged in through the door.

"*Mamá!* You're safe, thank goodness! What are you doing here?"

"Fernanda, my *cariña*, I was wondering where you were!"

Elliot couldn't take his eyes off Fern. Her cheeks were red and her eyes bright. She'd never been more beautiful in her life.

"*Mamá*, please get off that thing. It's dangerous!"

Elliot cleared his throat and stepped forward.

"Rosita, my name is Elliot," he said. "*Baje por favor, su hija está muy preocupada.*" He glanced at Fern, who was staring at him, open-mouthed. "*Estas segura aqui.*"

*Please come down, your daughter is worried. You are safe here.*

Rosita smiled brightly at Elliot. "*You are so handsome,*" she answered in Spanish. "*Is Hank here? Has he found us?*"

Elliot shook his head, assuring Rosita that Hank wasn't there. He'd started connecting the dots, figuring Hank had to be the man who'd hurt them all.

"*Hank isn't here. He won't ever harm you again,*" he said to Rosita determinedly.

Elliot knew now he would be here for Fern and Rosita, no matter what. He wasn't going to keep Fern at arm's length anymore, trying to guard his heart. She needed him.

Finally, he was willing to admit that he needed her, too.

Rosita climbed off the pedestal, and Elliot held out his hand to steady her. When she reached the floor, Fern flew into her mother's arms.

"I was so worried, *Mamá*! I thought something terrible happened to you."

"Nothing terrible happened, *cariña*. We are together, and that's all that matters."

Fern nodded, holding onto her mom as if she was scared that Rosita would fly away if she let her go.

"Will you let someone look at you?" Fern finally asked, letting go of Rosita.

Rosita pulled a face. "I don't like it when they look at me. Dr. Kirkland is very far away."

"It's just to be sure you're okay," Fern pleaded. "I'll call Dr. Kirkland and ask if someone close can help."

Rosita wanted to protest, but Elliot stepped closer.

"It's only because Fern cares that she's asking, Rosita," he said. "She had a terrible scare. You are the most important person to her."

Rosita looked at Elliot and smiled. "She's always cared so good for me. She's been so brave, my *querida niña*. I named her Fernanda for that, you know. It means 'brave,' and that's all she's been, fighting the terrible darkness that's been in our lives because of the choices I made."

Rosita's eyes became misty, and when Elliot looked at Fern, her eyes were also welling with tears.

"*Mamá,* I didn't know..."

"You have always been the pillar of strength, Fernanda. I know it's been difficult, but I've always seen you." She cupped her daughter's cheeks, and the two women hugged again.

Tears flowed freely. Elliot felt a lump in his throat, and when he looked at Thatcher and Veronica, who had stepped back to give the two women their moment together, they stood arm in arm, looking emotional, too.

Finally, Fern let go of her mom and stepped back. "Let me call Dr. Kirkland," she said. "Will you take care of her while we wait?" she asked Elliot, who nodded right away.

He would do anything and everything for Fern. She'd crept into his heart, and she was there to stay. He already had a soft spot for Rosita, too, and had a newfound respect for Fern now that he'd started to see how she looked after her mother and tried to protect her. Their situation was so much more than just one person being abused, and his heart went out to both of them.

The protector in him would do what needed to be done. He wasn't going to fight it anymore.

Fern turned away to call the doctor. Veronica jumped into action, making tea and coffee for everyone in the staff room while Rosita told Elliot and Thatcher everything about the art Fern had done since she was a child. Elliot loved listening to the older woman speak—the Spanish lilt in her accent was pleasant, and she talked about Fern with such reverence and affection. Elliot could listen to the woman all day.

Finally, Fern returned with news. An ambulance would come for Rosita and take her to a facility in Rockport, where they would make sure she was alright. Elliot helped Fern explain it to Rosita in a way that she agreed to go.

By the time the ambulance arrived, Rosita and Fern smiled at each other, the bond between them looking stronger than ever.

Fern looked lost when the ambulance drove away. She wrapped her arms around her body as if trying to physically keep herself together.

Elliot went to her. "Are you okay?"

When Fern leaned toward him, he put his arm around her shoulders. She leaned her head against him, and having her in his arms felt like the most natural thing in the world.

"I think so," she said. "I'm worried about her."

"She'll be safe," Elliot said. "You take very good care of her."

Fern nodded. "I didn't realize she'd seen everything I did all these years."

"You do more, and you are more than you realize," Elliot said softly. "Will you let me take you home?"

"I have nowhere to go," Fern said. "I gave up the Airbnb."

"Let me book you and your mom a room in my hotel until you find your feet," Elliot suggested.

Fern nodded. Before they left, she walked back into the studio and talked to Veronica. Elliot watched their conversation through the window, not wanting to go in and intrude. Whatever they were saying, Veronica was nodding and smiling, and Fern looked relieved. Finally, they hugged before Fern returned to Elliot outside.

"We can go," she said.

Elliot followed Fern the short distance to the hotel, where he booked a room for her and Rosita. He helped Fern carry her luggage into the room. When she sank onto the bed, she looked lost again.

"It's going to be okay," Elliot said, sitting down next to her.

"How do you know?"

"The worst is over, isn't it? You found your mom, she's in good hands, and you're together. You're here with people who care about you, and no matter what happens, you'll always have me in your corner."

"I can't tell you what a help you've been, talking my mom down like that."

"It was just a matter of making her feel safe and secure. I know a little about what fear can do to a person."

Fern swallowed hard, looking at her hands in her lap.

"I also know that when the fear is gone, a whole life blossoms into existence." He put his hand under her chin and gently lifted her face so she would look at him. "Your fear and your past don't define you, Fern. They're only a part of your life. You're bigger than that, better than that, and you're incredibly strong. Brave, too, just like your mother said."

Fern blushed lightly and a small smile played around her lips.

"I meant it when I said I would always be here for you."

Fern nodded, and Elliot leaned in closer. When she didn't pull away, he kissed her. She kissed him back, leaning toward him, and his heart sang. As long as they were together, they could face whatever came.

"I noticed you took those letters with you," Elliot said when they broke the kiss.

Fern nodded. "Strangely, holding onto those letters gave me the courage to stand up and face Hank. I just kept thinking, life is too short to let the bad things rule."

"It is," Elliot agreed. "I've had the same kind of epiphany, although not exactly like that."

"There's only one letter left I haven't read. I'm scared to open it—I'm terrified it will tell me those two people never found their happy ending."

"Why don't we read it together?" Elliot asked.

Fern nodded and stood, finding the last letter at the bottom of the bundle.


*My darling,*


*I don't know what life will hold for us. I don't know what the future will be. All I know is that this life is bland and colorless without you, and I have no interest in it. They say you don't know what you had until it's gone, but that's not true. I know exactly what we had. I made the mistake of thinking I could brave life without it.*

*I know now that I was so very wrong.*

*Where are you? What are you doing? I sincerely hope you've found some form of happiness in this new life we've created without each other. It's the only thing that might still bring me joy because I haven't found my happiness, and I don't think I ever will.*

*I miss you every day, and that will never change. I'll write every day, even if you don't read my letters.*

*I'll never stop loving you.*

*Yours always,*
*M.*

Fern lowered the letter, frowning.

"That's unsatisfying," she said. "I was hoping they ended up together. Or even if they didn't, I hoped this would be the end of the story. There are no answers here. It's only more of the same."

Elliot nodded, feeling the same disappointment. Deep down, he'd also hoped for closure.

"We'll just have to write our own story," he said firmly. "One that ends better than this."

"How?" Fern asked. "You're leaving soon."

"I'm not," Elliot said. "I've decided to stay. Moving away was the wrong thing to do. So, I'm here, and we're starting our lives together today. This is our happy ending in progress."

Fern smiled at him. "I like that."

Elliot returned the smile. He liked it very much, too.

# Chapter 19
# Fern

After Rosita returned from the hospital with a thumbs-up from Dr. Alford, the doctor who'd been recommended by Dr. Kirkland, Fern found that she could breathe again.

Her mother was in better spirits than she'd ever been. She was chatty and happy, and her eyes were clear—the cloudiness of delirium was absent. It had been years since Fern had seen her mother like this.

Now was the time to talk to her about Hank. It was now or never. She didn't know when she would find her mother in this clear state of mind again.

"*Mamá*, you have to leave Hank," she said, broaching the topic after a roundabout conversation. She had to be frank with her mother now. "He's not good for you, or for me. He's not good for *us*. He only causes pain and suffering, and life with him isn't what either of us deserves."

Rosita sighed. "I know. You're right. I was too scared of a life without him, and I let it go on for far too long. This wasn't the life I envisioned for us when I met him, you know. After your father left, I thought Hank could fill the gap and be the man we both needed. I was wrong. It would have been better to stay alone."

Fern shook her head. "Don't blame yourself for any of this. It was a very long, difficult time, and I understand why you decided to be with Hank. But it's time to move forward. I told Hank we're done with him, and I want you to embrace that. It might be hard, learning to do it all over again without anyone but the two of us...but we're not alone here. If coming to Waterstead taught me anything, it's that there are good people in the world. We must search until we find them and not settle for anything less."

Rosita cupped Fern's cheek. "You've grown, Fernanda. You've become strong and wise. You're right." She took a shuddering breath. "It won't be hard. I know I'm a burden to you, and—"

"You're not a burden to me," Fern interrupted. "You're my mother, and I love you. Hank was the burden, and without him, we can do this. I don't know where or how yet, but we'll figure that out."

Rosita nodded. Fern had already pored over listings for a place to stay in Waterstead. She desperately wanted her mother here with her. She'd fallen in love with the town and its people and didn't want to leave.

The small town didn't have any vacancies, and the studio apartment she would have rented from Veronica was much too small for her and her mother—they each needed a room of their own.

The phone rang, and Elliot's name flashed on the caller ID.

"Good morning," he said with a smile in his voice when she picked up. "How are you feeling today? How is Rosita doing?"

"We're okay," Fern said, and she was being honest—they may not be good just yet, but they were getting there. "As soon as I get my mom settled, I think things will start getting much better."

"We'll have to push for that, then," Elliot said.

Fern's heart sank. "I wanted to talk to you about that...I don't think we can stay in Waterstead."

"What?" She heard the disappointment and confusion in Elliot's voice.

"I'm sorry. There just isn't any space for us here, and I won't leave my mother alone again. I must think of her and put the two of us first for a change. It's been too long that I haven't done it, and we both need stability." *Even if it's without you*, she added silently. Saying the words out loud would break them both.

Elliot was quiet for so long, she wondered if he was still there.

"I understand," he finally said, although he sounded like he didn't understand at all. "I want the best for the two of you, no matter what it takes."

Fern smiled sadly. "You're a wonderful man, Elliot. I can't thank you enough for what you've done for us."

"It's only been my pleasure," Elliot said softly before they ended the call.

Fern lowered the phone to her lap. She knew she was doing the right thing by caring for her mother, by putting the two of them first. They had to get away from Hank, and this was the way to do it. She hated that she was sacrificing yet another thing for it, but this time, it was her choice.

"You'll miss him," Rosita said. She'd been reading in a chair by the window, and Fern hadn't realized she was listening to the conversation.

"I will," Fern admitted.

"He's a good man."

"He's the kindest and best of men," Fern agreed. "But our lives will become full and safe again, and the right people will cross our path as they should. I'll keep holding onto that."

"You've become so wise, like I've said before," Rosita said, turning her attention back to her book.

Fern smiled, basking in the compliment from her mom when she was so coherent.

"I have to talk to Veronica," Fern said, standing. "Will you be okay here?"

"I'll be fine," Rosita said.

Fern hesitated. "You won't leave and wander around?"

Rosita shook her head. "I'm where I belong, *cariña*. Go, and know that when you return, I'll be here, waiting for you."

Fern nodded, accepting that her mother would stay put. She walked to Rosita and kissed her forehead before she left the hotel room.

Her heart was heavy when she climbed into her car and drove to V Studios. The letter she and Elliot had read together was still on her mind. This was exactly what would happen to them—she and Elliot would have to be apart, and she would sacrifice a life with him. She understood now that things like this happened, though. Maybe it was what had happened to that couple, too.

Veronica was in V Studios scribbling on a piece of torn paper with a broken piece of charcoal. Fern couldn't help but smile—this was how she and Veronica had first met. Sadness came with the fond memory. She would have to leave all of this behind for good.

"Oh, you're here," Veronica said brightly when the bell jingled. "I was just thinking, we should settle the students according to—"

"I can't stay, Veronica," Fern said, getting straight to the point before Veronica shared all her plans for Fern's future at V Studios.

"What?" Veronica asked, confused. "I just got you back."

Fern nodded. "I know. I want to stay so badly, believe me. But I can't find a place to live for me and my mom here in Waterstead, and I won't leave her alone again. I must find a place where she can be safe and where we can both start over. I hoped it would be here, but..." Her voice trailed off as her emotions threatened to take over.

Veronica looked upset. "You belong here, Fern. We all know it. You weren't brought here by chance."

Fern nodded. "I know. I believe in fate, too. It just isn't allowing me to stay here. But so much has changed for the better that I can't be upset about how things are working out. My mom is more important to me than fighting the powers that be."

The more she talked about leaving, the sadder she became. She just wanted to say her goodbyes so she could go before becoming downright depressed about it. Leaving Waterstead behind was already tougher than she'd thought it would be.

"What if you can find a place here that works for you both?" Veronica asked. "Will you stay?"

"In a heartbeat," Fern said. "I love it here. This is home."

"We'll change the studio apartment upstairs."

"What?" Fern asked, confused.

"Elliot is a whiz, we've seen that. We'll make some additions and change the studio apartment into a two-bedroom place so you both can live there."

"Are you sure?" Fern asked.

"Of course! Thatcher will agree. I won't even have to ask, and it's an excuse to keep Elliot around, too." Veronica winked at Fern.

"You would do that for me?" Fern asked, dumbfounded.

"Of course. We care a lot more about you than you realize, Fern. We want you here, and we believe this is the right place for you. We'll make it work, whatever it takes."

Fern's eyes welled with tears all over again. She'd cried so much the last few days, not believing how many things were falling into place for her and Rosita.

"Thank you," she whispered, not trusting her voice if she spoke any louder.

Veronica pulled her into a hug. "We're happy to have you. You always have a job here, too. I want you to keep working at the studio."

Fern nodded. She would do it—all of it. She couldn't think of a fuller life than being in Waterstead, manning the studio and teaching art, with her mother safe and sound by her side.

When she left the studio, Veronica felt lighter than air. Laughter bubbled up in her throat. She couldn't believe how everything had worked out!

She had to find Elliot and tell him the news.

Just as she thought it, his truck pulled up next to her car. He jumped out of the truck, the engine still running.

"I'll do it," he said, out of breath.

"Do what?" she asked, confused.

"Move. To wherever you're going. Houston? I'm there. Miami, Chicago, anywhere. I'll follow you to the ends of the earth. If you can't be here, then I don't want to be, either."

"Are you serious?" Fern asked, stunned.

"I'm more serious about this than anything."

"You said you didn't want to move."

"I don't want to lose you. Nothing else matters."

Fern smiled, her cheeks burning. "I'm staying."

Elliot only stared at her.

"Veronica is making more work for you," she continued. "She's going to ask you to change the studio apartment into a two-bedroom place so my mom and I can live there and don't have to leave again. I'm not going anywhere. I was just on my way to tell you that."

Elliot's face brightened with surprise and joy before he

pulled Fern into a hug and spun her around. She laughed as he did.

"I'm in love with you, Fern," Elliot said. "I would follow you anywhere, and I can't tell you how happy I am that you're staying. I'm moving here, too."

Fern laughed. She thought the happiness would swallow her whole. She'd never felt this positive about the future.

"I'm in love with you, too. I can't think of a better place to be than right here, with you."

Elliot kissed her before he let go of her and spun her around again.

"I have something for you," Fern said when he finally set her down.

"For me?"

She nodded, beckoning him to follow her. They climbed the stairs to the studio apartment, and she unlocked the two doors. Once inside, she lifted the canvas with the ocean scene she'd painted for Elliot. Painting it felt like a lifetime ago now. It was hard to think it had just been a few nights ago.

"I know you wanted to talk about what you had in mind first, but this flowed freely when I painted, and I want you to have it."

"It's incredible," Elliot breathed, looking at the spectacular ocean view with the dark storm clouds.

"Now that you're staying at the coast, it's not quite so powerful since you'll see the ocean every day, but—"

"I love it," Elliot said. "Thank you."

Fern nodded and beamed. Everything was working out just as it should.

---

Elliot made quick work of the studio apartment. Everyone jumped in to help clean it—Veronica and Fern sorted through the last of the things, and Elliot and Thatcher worked together to get the bedroom partitions ready in record time. Even Rosita helped, dusting and wiping down furniture and decorating the space so it was ready for them to move in as soon as possible.

Since Fern had decided to stay in Waterstead and Rosita had agreed that leaving Hank was for the best, Rosita had been clear-minded and positive. She hadn't had an episode again, and the doctors all agreed that her environment was a big part of why.

If this was what being at the coast did for her mother, Fern would stay here forever. Not that she planned on leaving at any point.

Soon, once this was all taken care of, she would have to go back to Houston to collect her mother's things. She was terrified of doing that—it had a finality to it that scared her, although she knew it was the right thing to do. She was also worried about Hank and what he might do.

Elliot had offered to go with her, and she was grateful to him. She needed him to help her through the final push.

Elliot had seen a lot of ugly sides of Fern, but he was still there. He hadn't ditched her, hadn't once made her feel like she was a nuisance because of her past that still reared its ugly head at times. She was so grateful for him and the life they could live together now.

Elliot had found a place in Waterstead to live to be closer to Rosita and Fern. He still had his business in Rockport, and a manager who ran it. Elliot would drive out there if he needed to, and they would do business in the area. But Waterstead would be his home.

Fern couldn't be happier.

When she and Rosita stopped in front of Veronica's and Thatcher's beach house, a rumbling bark sounded from inside.

"What on earth is that?" Rosita asked, alarmed.

"That's Buster, *Mamá*. Brace yourself."

Before Rosita could respond, the large dog ran straight at her and jumped up on her. She and Fern took on the dog together. Buster licked Rosita's face with his pink tongue.

"Buster!" Thatcher shouted, running toward them from the house, Elliot right on his heels. "Get down, you big teddy bear!"

The two men wrestled Buster down and Fern looked at her mother, worried. But Rosita wasn't hurt at all. Instead, she was laughing.

"I love him!" She kneeled, hugging Buster. He sat happily, his tongue lolling out to the side, pleased that his efforts had gotten him so much affection.

Elliot and Thatcher smiled at the picture, and Fern took Elliot's hand and squeezed it.

"Are you ladies hungry?" Thatcher asked. "Veronica is whipping up a storm in that kitchen, and Elliot and I were about to put meat on the barbeque."

"Starving," Rosita said. "We're just in time for the magical sunset, too."

Fern nodded, and they all walked toward the beach house together.

Elliot took Fern's hand, and everything was perfect.

# Chapter 20
# Elliot

He drove to the studio apartment almost two months later, smiling from ear to ear. He'd finally finished the project at Thatcher's house, and everything looked just how the man had envisioned it. Elliot was pleased with his handiwork.

Since deciding to move to Waterstead, he'd started looking around for places to live. Fern had been right when she'd said there was no place to stay around these parts, and Elliot was trying to work out how he would commute from Rockport every day to see Fern and Rosita and make sure everything was okay.

That was when Thatcher had told him that the other cottage on his property was still free, and he would be willing to rent it to Elliot.

Veronica lived in the less rundown of the two cottages. Thatcher hadn't meant to fix up the empty one right away, but Elliot had suggested that he renovate it at no charge in lieu of a couple of months' rent. The agreement had worked out right, and Elliot had never been happier. Not only was he living along the coast, but he was right on the water now, watching sunrises every morning that took his breath away. And he had a landlord who was also a good friend.

He pulled up in front of V Studios. The bell jingled, announcing his arrival.

"Elliot," Veronica said with a smile. "What a pleasant surprise."

"It looks great in here," Elliot said, looking around the studio where new paintings had been displayed after many of the previous works had been sold.

Veronica nodded. "I don't know how I would have done it without Fern. She has a real eye for this stuff. I hired her to be a teacher and man the shop, but she keeps bringing so much more to the table. I think I'm going to push up her salary so she gets remunerated for how much she puts into the place."

Elliot smiled, proud of Fern. It had been a couple of weeks since she'd moved into the apartment upstairs. The longer she was away from the life she'd lived before, the more she opened up. He'd started seeing a side of her that had been hidden far, far away. She became more beautiful, more creative, more of everything that already defined her.

She still had moments when the past caught up with her, and Elliot could see the fear in her eyes. But those moments became fewer and further between as time marched on.

After Elliot had helped Fern retrieve her and Rosita's belongings from Houston, Fern had relaxed a lot more. She didn't need to look over her shoulder so much anymore. Elliot had learned much later that she'd been terrified of Hank coming to find her, that she'd run away from him and the abuse at home, and that was why she'd panicked when he'd arrived unexpectedly that morning.

Although she sometimes struggled, the larger part of her fear had subsided. When she did struggle, Elliot knew how to be there for her in a way that didn't make her feel threatened. Knowing how Tina had reacted after her abusive husband left had helped Elliot so much, enabling him to approach Fern's fears the right way.

Fern and Tina had met, too. Tina had been curious about the woman who'd stolen Elliot's heart. Once they'd gotten closer and Tina had confided in Fern about her own past, the women had struck an accord. They could relate to each other on a different level because of their mutual pain.

It made him happy that Fern and his sister got along so well. She had yet to meet his parents, but he wasn't in a hurry to go there. She got along with the one person who meant everything to him, and that was enough for now.

"Is Fern around?" Elliot asked Veronica.

She nodded. "Her class is just about wrapping up." She nodded toward the closed door that led to the back room. Fern had recruited a whole group of students and taught classes twice a week. The students loved her, and through word of mouth, she had twice as many sign-ups for the next course after this one finished.

"Do you want coffee while you wait?" Veronica offered.

Elliot nodded, and she disappeared into the staff room to make him a cup of coffee. He walked through the gallery, studying the paintings. Some of them had been created by Veronica herself; he recognized her style of abstract shapes and colors. Other artists' work also hung on the walls, and Elliot tilted his head this way and that, deciding how he felt about each of them.

Finally, he walked to the paintings Fern had created. He recognized her style immediately, and he relished the emotions she managed to evoke with her paintings of people and landscapes.

"Elliot," Fern said from behind him. He smiled before he turned.

She looked like a vision, her hair pulled back in a ponytail, with flyaway strands framing her face. She wore clothes stained with paint splotches, making her look like art herself. Her eyes were bright.

"How was your class?" he asked after pecking her on the lips. Fern's students passed behind them, waving at Fern before they left.

"It was good. They learn so fast! They have a lot of talent."

"I think they learn fast because you're a good teacher," Elliot said, smiling at her.

Fern giggled. "Flatterer. What are you doing here?"

"I wanted to tell you that I'm finished at Thatcher's place. It's done! I wanted to celebrate the end of a great project."

"You're completely done? Congratulations!"

"Thanks," Elliot beamed. "It's so much more satisfying this time around, but I think it's because I was so much more personally involved."

"The personal stuff is always so much bigger," Fern agreed.

"I also want to show you something. Do you have some time to get away?"

Veronica returned with the coffee she'd made for Elliot, and he thanked her for it. "Get away from what?" Veronica asked.

"I want to show Fern something, if she can break away for a quick moment," Elliot said.

"Oh, sure. Go on," Veronica said. "I've got the studio under control."

"You're sure?" Fern asked.

Veronica nodded. "You deserve a break away now and then. You work so hard."

Fern smiled and looked expectantly at Elliot. He gulped down the hot coffee before hurrying to the staff room to drop off his empty cup. When he came back to the gallery, Fern and Veronica immediately stopped talking as if they'd been discussing him. Fern's eyes glittered, her cheeks bright red. Whatever they'd said about him had been good.

"Ready?" he asked Fern.

They left the studio. He opened the passenger door to his truck for her, closing it behind her when she got in. He climbed behind the wheel and turned the ignition, pulling onto the road.

While he drove through town, Fern explained to him how her class had gone and what they'd covered in the lesson. He loved hearing her talk about her classes and the paintings she created. From the moment he'd met her, he'd found her passion contagious, and seeing her come to life was always a sight to behold.

"What are we doing here?" Fern asked with a frown when Elliot parked in front of Linda's haberdashery.

"This is what I want to show you," Elliot said.

"I don't understand."

"You will. Just follow me."

He ran around the truck and opened the door for Fern before leading her into the haberdashery. When the door jingled, Linda appeared from a back room.

"Oh, there you are," she said happily. "Come through."

Fern frowned at Elliot, but he gestured for her to follow Linda. The older woman led them to a back room where chairs had been set up in a circle. A tray of iced tea and cookies waited for them.

"Sit down, help yourself," Linda said.

"You didn't have to go to so much effort," Elliot said.

Fern still looked confused, but she accepted the iced tea he poured for her along with a small plate of cookies. She nibbled on one.

"After I finished Thatcher's project this morning, I went back to the cottage to collect the last box of things I wanted to donate," Elliot explained. "Linda went through it with me, and that letter we read in the hotel the other day was in it. I don't know how it ended up between those things, but..." He glanced at Linda to continue the story.

"When I saw the letter, it brought me back to a very dark time in my life," she said. "I told you about the love of my life when I was younger, how it never worked out, but I ended up happy with Patrick."

Fern nodded.

"Well, my first love and Patrick are one and the same."

Fern looked confused. "I don't understand."

"That brooch...Patrick gave it to me when we were young and in love, but circumstances pulled us apart. We couldn't be together, and we both decided it was for the better...well, I should say he decided it was for the better if we were apart. I wasn't so happy with that. I was willing to sacrifice everything to go after him, no matter where he went. I was ready to give up my studies, my family, my dreams. He wouldn't let me. He said it wasn't right that I give up my life for him, that it had to go both ways if we were to be together forever. I threw that brooch at him in anger that day."

"The chip in the ivory you were telling me about is from that," Fern said in realization.

Linda nodded. "We were apart for months. It was torture, as I'm sure you could figure out from the letters we wrote each other. I spent nights crying myself to sleep and days on autopilot, going through the motions because what else was I supposed to do? I'd lost the love of my life. No other man was worth my time, no one caught my eye, and I resolved to live the rest of my life a spinster if I couldn't have him." Her eyes became misty. "This letter..." She picked up the letter from the table. "This was the last letter I ever wrote him."

"What happened?" Fern asked, completely engrossed in the story. Elliot listened intently, too. Linda had given him an overview, but the details were new to him.

"He came for me." Linda smiled a smile of pure happiness. "He was the one who told me he couldn't live without me, and he'd given everything up to be with me instead. A life without each other was no life at all."

Fern shook her head. "The letters don't finish. We thought the story never ended, or if it did, we didn't know how."

"The letters don't finish because from that day on, we were inseparable. There was no reason to keep writing to each other because we were together. We got married, and we were never apart a single day until the day my dear Patrick passed away." Tears rolled down Linda's cheeks, and she pressed the letter to her chest and closed her eyes. "I still miss him every day, but the pain is different now. We had a full life together. For forty-five years, I woke up to him every morning and went to bed with him by my side every night. He was my first hello and my last goodbye."

She opened her eyes again, and they filled with affection. "Can I keep this letter?"

"Oh, you can have all of them!" Fern cried out. "Right, Elliot? We'll give you every letter we found."

"I'd love to hold onto them. They're a memory of my Patrick," Linda said.

Fern nodded, and Elliot did, too. It was only right that the letters were returned to their rightful owner.

"There's just one last thing I don't understand," Fern said. "Your letters...they're all signed with the letter M."

Linda smiled. "My full name is Melinda."

The rest of the afternoon was an emotional one. Linda told them stories of the adventures she and Patrick had gone on after getting married, of the children that had grown up and moved away, and how they'd settled in Waterstead when they retired. Listening to Linda speak with so much affection warmed Elliot, and every time he glanced at Fern, he knew their story was as special as Linda's and Patrick's.

Finally, when the sun started to set and dusk crept into the room, it was time to go. Elliot and Fern both thanked Linda.

"You're more than welcome," she said. "Thank you so much for returning my letters to me. Just remember, when you find your person, hold onto them forever. It only happens once in a lifetime, and life without that kind of love just isn't worth it."

Elliot and Fern glanced at each other before they nodded and smiled at Linda. They left the store and got into Elliot's truck.

He drove Fern back to the studio, but they sat in the truck in silence long after the engine shut off.

"Thank you for taking me to see Linda," Fern finally said. "I can't tell you what it means that we know how the story ended, and that it ended well."

"It means a lot to me, too. It's such a happy ending."

"I love happy endings," Fern said with a smile.

Elliot put his arm around Fern's shoulders and pulled her a little closer.

"I love happy endings, too," he said. "And...I love you."

Fern glanced up at him. It was the first time he'd said those words rather than telling her he was *in* love with her.

She smiled at him, running her hand over his cheek.

"I love you, too," she said.

He dropped a kiss into her hair, and they sat together as night fell.

# About the Author

Eliza's a BIG believer in love. She writes sweet romances that make you swoon, laugh and believe in love again.

A mother of two children, Eliza and her husband of twenty-five years live in NH. She enjoys spending time with them and taking care of her many pets. When she isn't working on her next book, you can find her at the local nursery looking for the next hybrid tea rose to add to her garden.

**Stay up to date with
Eliza's new releases, discounts and more!**
www.ElizaEster.com/mail